# Praise for Corey Mesler

"It's no secret that Corey Mesler is one hell of a writer. The irresistible *Camel's Bastard Son* is his tenth novel. One marvel of this gritty and propulsive tale is its bravado. There aren't many writers who would dare to do what Corey does here. He explores a wild new territory of desperate love, alienation, heartache, and . . . well, let's just say, you're about to travel to places you've never been before. Billy Kos, as memorable a character as you're likely to meet, has embarked on a long strange trip, and there's room for one more. So hop aboard, but strap on your seatbelt and hold on to your hat. The road's a little bumpy up ahead."
—John Dufresne, author of *Louisiana Power and Light* and *I Don't Like Where This Is Going*

"Corey Mesler has written a dystopian novel for the post-Trump era, giving us an imagined world—actually, an imagined universe—populated with a cast of characters who seem too far-fetched for today but eerily plausible for the not-too-distant future. If this a nightmare (or, "daymare," as Mesler calls it) about where we're headed, the novel makes a poignant, often-funny plea for changing direction."
—Dana Sachs, author of *The Secret of the Nightingale Palace* and *If You Lived Here*

"*Camel's Bastard Son*, by Corey Mesler, is smart, sharp, weird, sexy and funny, which is to say it's terrific, and I read it at a gallop, and I'm betting you will too. This is like Kurt Vonnegut for our fraught moment. It's also—hats off to Mesler—like nothing I've ever read."
—Laird Hunt, author of *The Impossibly* and *In the House in the Dark of the Woods*

# CAMEL'S BASTARD SON

Corey Mesler

CABAL BOOKS
ST PAUL, MN

CAMEL'S BASTARD SON



ISBN: 978-0-9996716-4-1

First paperback edition published by Cabal Books
February 2020



www.cabalbooks.us

Cover design by Karly Andersen
Cover painting, Grace, by Nancy Cheairs
Typeset by Michael Kazepis

Cabal Books
DBA Thicke & Vaney Books
P. O. Box 16305
St. Paul, MN 55116

*for Cheryl, who is the past present and future of me*

Humanity is sick and tired of being what it is. It's always wanted to escape from its state of being—into the ocean seas, the Indies, the frontier, the New Frontier, space, the life hereafter, war—anything to kill the boredom.

—Charles McCarry

Something opens our wings. Something
makes boredom and hurt disappear.

—Rumi

# PRELUDE

## From Wikipedia, the free encyclopedia:

Camel Jeremy Eros (born July 20, 1935 [in some reference works 1941]) was an American writer, born in Memphis, Tennessee. Perhaps best known as a poet (habitually associated with the San Francisco Renaissance and the protests of the 1960s). He was the son of renowned jazz artists Axel and Maya Revel Eros. He was married to artist and sculptor Allen Fermor Eros, who died December 8th, 1980, the same day as John Lennon. Her death formed a dark cloud over Camel's remaining days and, some believe, he was celibate until late in life, when he took up with a much younger woman, whose name, curiously, seems to have been Lorax. Little is known of her. He has been described as the "poet laureate of pussy and protest." Eros is a winner of a Pulitzer Prize for Poetry (posthumous) and the American Book Award for his sixth book, A Small Period of Relief. His work moves easily from beat narrative to surrealism to love poems and poems about nature. Camel Eros has been translated into numerous languages, including Japanese, possibly because of his connection with hippie poet, Richard Brautigan. For many years, Eros served as a faculty member at Memphis State, alongside poets Gordon Osing and

Pinter Monk. After a lifetime spent in both San Francisco and New York he settled in his hometown of Memphis in his thirties and stayed there, nearly a recluse, until his death in 2008 at the age of 73 [or 67]. He and Allen never had children but there is an unsubstantiated report that he fathered an illegitimate son by, some say, a young woman from his highschool days, while others say an older woman who was a friend of his wife's.

# PART ONE: EARTH

The future has an ancient heart.
—Carlo Levi

The greatest saving one can make in the order of thought is to accept the unintelligibility of the world—and to pay attention to man.
—Albert Camus

## CHAPTER ONE

In grade school, when Billy Kos began writing poems, he thought something had gone wrong within himself. If Jack or Rob or Kicky found out he was toast. They were not appreciators of verse. They were kids from bad neighborhoods whose idea of fun was shooting their neighbors' pets with pellet guns.

Billy Kos just wanted to fit in. This was suburban America. Fitting in was fairly easy if you turned your imagination off. Billy had an imagination as large as a European country. Ordinarily, however, this did not make him a poet. It made him a dreamer and a smartass. It made him answer the teacher's inevitable question, "Billy, are you paying attention?" this way: "I am paying more than it's worth."

Billy Kos was popular because of this ability. Once past the part of life where it was more important to use one's fists Billy had a number of nice, untroubled years, enjoying his newfound power as Class Clown. Rita Someback thought he was the shits. Billy knew this because Helen Holland told him, "Rita Someback thinks you're the shits."

Billy had been around enough to know that this was a good thing. He was fifteen. He also knew he could probably see Rita Someback's wee breasties if he played his cards right. This was something he desired very much to see. So, after school one day, Billy asked Rita if she wanted to walk out to the baseball field and sit in the dugout with him. This was a notorious necking spot. Rita tilted her sparkly little face upward and said, "Billy Kos I'd love to sit in the dugout with you."

That afternoon the walk to the dugout was slow and painful. Rita talked as if she hadn't talked for months and decided to unloose all that pent-up language on Billy. Billy only half-listened. He was thinking about undoing Rita's brassiere if she wore one over her wee breasties. He knew little about brassieres. Rita's run-on monologue was tinny background music to Billy's wriggling fantasy.

"Billy, are you listening to me?" Rita stopped on the pitcher's mound to ask.

Billy stopped also.

"Of course I am, Rita. Your brother is thinking about joining the Navy Seals."

"Billy Kos. I don't have a brother. I was talking about Easter Seals. It's my favorite charity." Here Rita paused and slapped Billy with a paperback copy of *Romeo and Juliet*. "What's your favorite charity?"

Billy squinted at the far horizon. He reconfigured his face into the face of a man who thought deep thoughts. "I think probably the United Negro Collage Fun."

Rita laughed. She thought Billy had made a joke because Billy was the Class Clown.

Once in the dugout (finally, Billy thought) Rita grew quiet. She was waiting to be kissed. She looked like she might have been kissed before. This emboldened young Billy Kos.

"Hey Rita," he said. "Since there's no one around how about you show me your tits?"

This time Rita used her balled up hand, which made a fist about the size of a kiwi, to punch Billy Kos right in the nose.

"Dammit," Billy said, grabbing his offended snout. He didn't even have time to add, "We can do something else," because Rita Someback was across that infield faster than a Wade Boggs grounder.

## CHAPTER TWO

Unfortunately, this set up a sad template for Billy's future dealings with women. In college he dated a few women *once*—or twice if the first date was somewhat ambiguous—but no one ever wanted to see him more than this. He hadn't been punched in the snout again but his ego took quite a beating.

Then, during his senior year at The University of Memphis, shortly before he was to graduate with a C- average from the anthropology department (Billy knew nothing about anthropology—not even the meaning of the word—when he picked it as his major from a list his advisor showed him because it was the 2nd choice on the list and the 1st would make him seem to be picking his future at random, and only a little bit more when he graduated) he met Kalma Voyles. She was sitting in the student center, alone in front of a TV showing a soap opera, her books strewed around her ankles as if she had just dropped them there, which she had. Kalma had a slight overbite, full lips which she was in the habit of tugging on, an overabundance of freckles and the glassy-eyed look of the inbred. She also had the best legs Billy had ever seen, and they were fully on display because Kalma Voyles sat slouched in the sling-back chair, her legs akimbo and her skirt hiked up her thighs, revealing not only shapely gams but bright yellow panties.

From fifty yards away Billy Kos fell in love with her in a heartbeat.

He was, for the first time since high school, driven to attempt a poem. It was called "Kalma's Yellow Panties," and, thankfully, it is lost to history. Billy himself forgot it except for one line which he used to woo her: "Her legs were the apotheosis of legs/between them the color of jaundice."

It happened this way: that very first sighting (panties! the grade-schooler inside him crowed) emboldened Billy Kos and he slowly approached as if she were a skittish hart and might dart away. He was impelled forward as his eyes attempted to penetrate that golden space in the middle of Kalma Voyles.

"What are you watching?" Billy said when he was only two steps away.

Kalma Voyles slowly turned her head, her attention reluctantly drawn away from her show. Billy Kos seemed to tower over her as if a giant, but it was only because he was standing too close.

"Wha?" Kalma said.

"The television. What's on?" Billy was now looking at her face close-up. He loved the freckles, the deep philtrum, and those lips as full as a pink summer rose, and roughly that hue. He loved Kalma Voyles before he even knew her name.

Kalma Voyles pulled on her lower lip and then released it the way one does a blind.

"Soap opera," Kalma said. She turned back to the TV and forgot instantly the man standing too close to her.

Normally Billy would have run. He didn't want his nose punched again.

"My name's Billy," Billy Kos said. He didn't mean to speak to this vision as if she were five years old. "What's your name?"

"Huh?" Kalma said, without turning his way again.

Billy, indeed, had to persevere. He had to cut through the thicket of her indifference.

"My name is Billy Kos."

He let silence reign. The TV went to a commercial.

Kalma Voyles turned toward Billy again.

"Could you step back a bit?" she asked.

"Of course," Billy said, gallantly.

"What do you want?"

"To know you. To talk to you. To carry your books home from school." He thought this last bit was the height of wit.

"I have my own car," Kalma said.

Billy had to think fast. TV commercials don't last forever, even if they seem to.

"Would you like to go out with me tonight?"

Kalma blinked a few times. She pulled her lip. She reached down and pulled her skirt over her thighs. She rose.

"You want to ask me for a date?"

"Yes," Billy said. He smiled like James Garner.

"You don't know me," Kalma said.

"I know. I want to correct that."

"Why?"

"To see what follows. To test the present against the future."

Kalma Voyles still didn't understand. "I still don't understand," she said.

"A date. The movies maybe. Dinner out. You know, like people do."

"Ok, I guess," Kalma said.

"Great. Great," Billy Kos said. "Let's go out to eat. That way we can talk more."

"Yeah, ok," Kalma said.

"Here, write down your address."

Billy handed her a pen and the torn-off corner of a page from his copy of *Outlines and Highlights for Exploring Biological Anthropology.*

Kalma wrote her address down. Number, street, city and zip code.

"Thank you," Billy Kos said.

The soap opera returned. Kalma's attention left Billy.

Billy looked at the paper, then at Kalma's face, then at the TV, then at Kalma's thighs, which were re-spread, then back at the paper, then back at Kalma's face.

"I didn't get your name," he said.

"Kalma," said, without turning.

"Kalma," Billy said it, half under his breath.

On the way home Billy said her name over and over. He went straight home and, after grabbing a piece of cake from the kitchen counter, he sprinted to his room and wrote "Kalma's Yellow Panties." He thought it was the best thing he'd ever written. It was—but the bar was set pretty low.

## CHAPTER THREE

Billy was on time picking her up. He was always on time, if not neurotically early. Kalma's duplex was off Southern Avenue, fairly close to the University of Memphis campus. On her door was a small wreath of plastic flowers, the kind of cheap stuff one finds at dollar stores.

Billy knocked. And waited.

Then he knocked again.

And waited. Finally, he heard someone fumbling with the bolts and locks. This took longer than was necessary, it seemed to Billy. The door was eventually opened and Kalma was standing there, dressed in a terrible pink housecoat.

"Oh!" she said.

"Am I early?" Billy asked, his smile a rictus.

"Tonight. We're going out to dinner." Kalma squinched her features up. "Yes," she finished.

"Right. Did you still want to go?"

"Sure, sure I do," Kalma answered. She shifted from one foot to the other. "Um," she said.

"Want me to wait out here?" Billy said without edge.

"Oh, no, you should come in."

Since she did not step aside Billy took a tentative step toward her.

"Oh, yes," Kalma said, and pressed her mouth against Billy's. Billy held on with his lips. His balance on the step was precarious. Kalma kept her full lips pressed against Billy's for about twenty seconds. Finally, she moved backwards.

"Whew," she said.

Billy smiled and stepped by her into the apartment. It was a sty. It was hard to see where papers and books and food packages ended and the furnishings began. There was a fermented tang in the air.

"Whew," Kalma said again. "Maybe it wasn't the right time for that."

"What?" Billy said. His mind's bobbery seemed to be drawing on the chaos of Kalma's living room.

"You kiss well," Kalma said.

"Oh, yes, thank you," Billy answered, turning back to his hostess.

"Now it's time to go out to eat," Kalma said. She pulled at her bottom lip.

"Yes, if you'd still like to," Billy said.

Kalma's face clouded. "Wait a sec, Buster, you think you're getting me into bed this quickly you better think again."

"No. I. What? I asked if you still wanted to go out to eat." Billy's irritation was growing. Should he just bolt? This woman was perhaps too odd, too *something*. Then he remembered those panties, those legs.

Kalma was standing still in her pose of defiance. Apparently, Billy was supposed to speak again.

"I didn't mean the alternative was sexual."

Kalma thought this over. "Ok," she said, brightening. "I'll get dressed."

She went down the hall running a slalom over piles of detritus. When she returned she was wearing jeans and a t-shirt with small birds appliqued on it.

The ride to the restaurant was achieved with only a modicum of peculiarity and Billy's confidence in the evening was renewed. They went to eat at an Italian restaurant in the Cooper Young neighborhood. It was pretty upscale and Billy fretted about his finances while they were eating. He had to focus his attention back on his date, whose freckled face made Billy's heart beat fast.

"This is a nice place," Billy said, after the waiter had taken their orders.

Kalma looked around. She made no comment.

"Do you like Italian?" Billy tried again.

"I like Mussolini," Kalma said.

Billy was sure he had heard wrong. A lacuna opened in the conversation. Billy dipped a piece of bread in the small dish of olive oil and ate it in one bite. Kalma watched him as if he were an ape at the zoo using sign language.

"Are you supposed to do that?" she asked.

"Yes," Billy told her. "It's olive oil."

When the food arrived the conversation became even smaller as they each ate. Kalma looked carefully at each forkful before putting it in her mouth, as if she were inspecting it for ricin or bugs. The meal took a long time. Billy tried to slow down to match her glacial pace. When the bill came Billy paid it. Kalma said 'thank you' to the waiter. They rose and left.

The ride back to Kalma's was very quiet. Kalma pulled at her lip.

Billy watched the road. Darkness had come on. He could not see her magnificent legs and he vowed he would chance a second date, no matter how difficult, in hopes that she would wear a dress.

Billy walked her to her door.

"Well," he said.

Kalma now stared at him as if seeing him for the first time. She was thinking about something.

"We already kissed," she said, at last.

"Yes," Billy said.

"And so now. . ."

Was she asking Billy what came next?

"I guess we could kiss again," she said.

"Yes," Billy said, stupidly. Kalma was one step higher than Billy and didn't seem willing to come down to his level. He tried to join her on the top step but it was too narrow. He lost his balance and barked his wrist against the door jamb.

"Ouch," Billy Kos said.

"Here," Kalma said, stepping down.

The kiss was long, very long in Billy's short history of bussing, and wet like an oasis, and Kalma even frenched his eager mouth a couple times before the break.

"Whew," she said again.

"Good night, Kalma. Would you like to go out again?"

"Not right now," Kalma said. "I hope the tongue was alright."

"Yes, I mean I meant another night."

"Oh, yes. I think that would be pleasant," Kalma said.

"When are you free?" Billy Kos asked, still tasting her tongue in his mouth.

"I'm always free," Kalma answered.

## CHAPTER FOUR

Billy Kos's best friend, at this crucial stage in his life, was a fellow student named Willie Waugh. Willie was a philosophy major and was under the mistaken impression that women liked smart men. Willie didn't give a damn about Kant or Wittgenstein or Bertrand Russell.

Neither of the friends minded when people laughed at the pairing of Billy and Willie. They felt it gave them a certain cache. Any attention was good attention.

Walking together to the campus cafeteria Billy wanted feedback from his pal about the new female in his life.

"She said 'I hope the tongue was alright'?" Willie asked for clarification.

"Yes, she has an odd way about her. She seems . . . *ethereal.*"

"Maybe she's retarded."

"They don't use that word anymore."

"Who doesn't?"

"They. The people who make the rules for society."

"I wish I was one of them."

"Yeah, me too."

"What's the new word?"

"The new word for what?"

"Retarded."

"I'm not sure. Slow? After ex-President Trump, rest in pieces, issued his edict banning intellectuals from public discourse some distinctions are . . . not so distinct."

"Maybe she's slow."

"I don't think so."

"Does she make smart conversation?"

"No, she doesn't make smart conversation, I wouldn't say."

"Maybe she's an alien."

"That's possible," Billy said. "She doesn't act like any earthling I've ever known."

"Of course, your dating record is, what should we say, a small sampling."

"Yes. Yours isn't much better."

"No, it isn't."

They said nothing more until they had their trays full and were seated in a corner of the cafeteria.

"Then why ask me for dating advice?" Willie asked, slathering a corn dog with mayonnaise.

"I think you're supposed to put mustard on those."

"Who says?"

"They do," Billy Kos said and both men laughed.

"So why, I repeat, ask me for dating advice?"

"Willie, who else? I'm not gonna ask my dad. He thinks since my mom died that there are no more women on the planet. Besides, you know, you don't talk to parents about sex."

"Have you already had sex with Velma?" Willie almost choked on a wee piece of wiener.

"Kalma. And, no. Not even close. Unless French kissing is sex."

"Closer than I've been in a while."

"Sorry, Willie."

"It's ok. No, it's not ok. Are you seeing Kalma again?"

"Yes, a second date. There's almost more pressure during a second date, I think."

"Another small sampling."

"Yes, that's true."

"Tell her about Kant. Women love smart men."

"I know nothing about Kant."

"Bertrand Russell?"

"Stop it. I don't need conversational fodder. I need—I am not sure what I need. To understand this woman, to know what she's thinking, to see if I rate at all with her."

"You're asking a lot."

"I know."

"You won't find out on a second date. Probably. At least I don't think so."

"What are you doing now?"

"What?"

"You're putting salt on your Fritos?"

## CHAPTER FIVE

Billy Kos did not have an original idea for a second date so he proposed dinner again. He hoped that after dinner they could go to her place and be alone for a while. He assumed she lived alone. And he couldn't very well ask her back to his house where he lived with his father.

This time Kalma came to the door right away. And she was wearing a short dress that showed off her immaculate thighs. Billy almost swooned.

Driving to the restaurant he could not keep his eyes off those leggy swells. They were like some living thing, an otter, or muskrat.

"What are you looking at?" Kalma asked.

"Sorry?"

"You better watch the road."

"Yes, yes," Billy said, blushing.

"Where are we going?"

"I thought Chinese tonight."

Kalma Voyles pulled on her bottom lip and stared out the windshield.

"Is that ok?"

"Hm?"

"Chinese?"

"Yes, I love Chinese food."

The dinner was brought promptly. The ambience of the restaurant was funky and tacky, cramoisy velvet curtains and plaster Buddhas. Billy had ordered cashew chicken and Kalma something with duck in it.

"This is especially good chicken," Billy said. "How's yours?"

"I didn't get chicken," Kalma said, spearing some strange vegetable as if she were gigging for frogs.

"Duck. How's your duck?"

"Have you ever eaten here before?"

"No, no I haven't. A friend recommended it. Do you not like it?"

"Do you have many friends?"

Billy's brain felt like the car on a roller coaster, heading toward steep drop-offs and jolting turns. Conversation with Kalma was full of oblivion-hahas.

"Sure, I have friends. Willie, he's a good friend."

"Billy and Willie."

"Yes, we get that a lot."

Kalma began to giggle. She giggled like a tap dripping. Then she began to laugh louder and had to put her fork down. Her laugh was like the crackling of artillery.

Billy watched her with pleasure. He fell in love with that laugh and then, just as suddenly, he thought he had fallen in love with Kalma Voyles.

The ride home was more convivial. Both smiled for whatever reasons and Billy kept stealing glances at those thighs.

"You're looking at my legs. That's what I just figured out," Kalma said.

Billy burned red and smiled an impish smile. He didn't know it was impish but it was.

"Do you want to come in?" Kalma asked at the door.

"I really do," Billy said.

Once inside it took Kalma several minutes to do whatever she was doing in her room and then in the kitchen. Billy sat on a sprung pleather couch which smelled faintly of cat pee. Kalma returned with glasses full of a purple liquid.

"Wine?" Billy asked.

"Kool-Aid."

"Ah. I love Kool-Aid." It was true, he really did.

"Me too. That's good, isn't it?"

"What's that?"

"That we have similar interests."

"Yes," Billy said, sipping. "What flavor is this?" "I like to mix. It's grape Kool-Aid and Rootin'-Tootin raspberry."

"Nicely done," Billy Kos said.

They were quiet for a while and Billy looked at the dim surrounding room. If one tried to create this much chaos in a room it couldn't be done. This was months of neglect.

"Do you want to look at my legs some more?" Kalma asked abruptly.

Billy coughed a fake cough into his fist. He'd seen someone do that on TV.

"Yes, I do," he said. "Your legs are as perfect as the stars."

"That's an odd thing to say. Are you a poet?"

"No, not really," Billy said. "I did write a little poem about you."

Kalma giggled again but this time it did not escalate.

"Her legs were champion/between them the color of jaundice," Billy quoted himself.

"Pardon?"

"That's from the poem. It's all I remember."

Kalma thought for a minute. "Say it again."

Billy did and Kalma thought for a minute more.

"Why jaundice?"

"Oh, nothing," Billy stammered. "Yellow. It means yellow. I use a thesaurus."

"Like my yellow panties."

Billy tried to swallow but he had a tumbleweed in his throat.

"Ok, you can look at my legs some more," Kalma said, as if the poem reaffirmed the decision for her.

Billy got his throat cleared. He fixed his eyes on Kalma's thighs like a man studying a new species in a petri dish. His gaze was intent, solemn.

"You look good," Kalma said.

"Oh, Kalma," Billy replied. "You look good, too. I could eat your thighs for dessert."

Kalma began to giggle and then cut it short. "I meant you are a good looker." She stifled half a giggle. "Wait, are we talking about sex now?"

Billy could not speak.

"I guess next you want to see my yellow panties."

For a second date, Billy was to say later, it was pretty first rate.

## CHAPTER SIX

In Human Adaptation class Billy Kos was having trouble concentrating. He had not slept at all the night before. Instead he watched Kalma sleep; a soft snore like a puppy whimper escaped her thick lips. Billy peeled the covers back and kept studying her body in the fuscous light from her Banana Splits night light. Her breasts were small and slightly uneven. Her stomach was flat and warm and as beautiful as a sheaf of wheat. Her pubic hair was thick, which Billy liked very much. And then her legs, her imperial legs.

"Mr. Kos must have studied deep into the night last night. He's in danger of dropping off the side of his desk," Professor Markson said. The class tittered. One would think college students, especially at this level, would be too detached to titter, but one would be wrong.

Billy smiled. Nothing could hurt him today. He was replaying the night on the second-run movie screen in his head.

Kalma was so odd, but Billy, with little to compare her to, was taken with her every jerk and quirk.

They had not had sex. In the cool light of day, it didn't seem as strange as it did at the time. Billy had not had sex in a long time and, once upon the brink, every fiber of his being joined in the parade to his genitals. And his genitals wanted, wanted, wanted.

"I do, um, want to see your yellow panties," Billy said, as the film re-commenced. Kalma had not even asked him how he knew she wore them.

"Ok, Billy Kos. Close your eyes."

Billy closed his eyes. He felt the loss of her weight on the couch next to him. He heard her shuffle through the debris. Then a silence that seemed to go on and on.

"Well don't you want to see them?" she asked.

Billy opened his eyes. Kalma was holding up a pair of yellow panties.

"They were in the wash," she said.

"Oh," Billy said. He wanted to go home.

"You act now like you don't like them as much," Kalma said, and she pulled her lip and frowned.

"They're lovely. Sometime . . . I'd like to see them on you." Was this too bold? Would she ask him to leave?

"Oh, sure, Billy Kos. Sure."

She came and sat back beside him.

"What color is your underwear?" she asked solemnly.

"Oh, uh, white, I feel sure."

"Ok," Kalma said.

"Well," Billy Kos said, exercising the time-tested cue for exits.

"Do you think I can see your underwear, Billy Kos?" Kalma said. There was no coyness, no lighthearted flirtatiousness. She asked as if she were a technician doing research.

"They're, that is, it's not, you know, very interesting," Billy said. He was confused.

"Ok. I thought we were talking underwear because you wanted to."

"No, I, Kalma, it's just that, you know—dammit, I find you so attractive," Billy stumbled.

Kalma pulled her lip. "You want to see the underwear I'm wearing." It was an asseveration not a question.

"You bet I do," Billy said, more forcefully. This wending conversation was frustrating him.

"At the same time," Kalma said.

"What?"

"At the same time. We show at the same time."

Billy was back in grade school.

"Kalma—"

"I'll count to three."

"Kalma, I—"

"One. . ." Kalma put her hands on the hem of her short skirt.

"Ok, wait, wait—"

"Two."

And Billy undid his belt and the snap on his jeans.

"And three."

Kalma lifted her dress right up over her face. Her panties were lizard green as was her matching bra. Billy's hand and heart stopped simultaneously. He stared.

"Oops," Kalma said. "I can't see you!" She dropped her skirt.

"Sorry—" Billy said. He unzipped and pulled his jeans down. They sat awkwardly looking at each other, Kalma's dress at half-mast and Billy's pants, ridiculously around his ankles.

"They are just white," Kalma said.

"Sorry. Disappointed?"

"I don't know, Billy Kos." Kalma's expression was unreadable, overly serious.

"You, you're beautiful," Billy said.

"Can I put my dress down now?"

"No," Billy Kos said.

"No?" Now Kalma smiled a wee smile. If she giggles, Billy thought, I'm going to pounce on her.

"Kalma, my melon," Billy said, stupidly.

Kalma did not giggle. She laughed that bright, brass bell laugh. Billy was in love.

Instead of pouncing Billy kicked off his shoes, stood and removed his jeans and then his shirt. He stood before her in his whites and his black socks. He was declaiming, without words, I will be naked for you.

"Ok," Kalma said. She stood and lifted the dress off over her head. Then she unsnapped her bra and let it fall, too.

"I think we should kiss now," Billy said.

"Yes, ok," Kalma said.

Billy put his hands on her ample waist and slowly leaned in. Her lips were open and soft and wet and her tongue immediately sought his. Kalma Voyles, for all her peculiarity, could really kiss. Billy's erection was pressed against her abdomen. She must have stood about 5'4" because Billy was 5'9". They kissed for a long time. Billy's heat was rising and he thought perhaps his love's was as well. They dropped sideways onto the couch and one of Billy's hands fell between the cushions. What it touched he did not want to see. It was foodish. Now their kiss grew more passionate. When Billy's tongue entered Kalma's mouth she sucked on it hard and her hands ran down his chest and into the hair around his navel. This is it, Billy thought. A handjob at least.

Instead Kalma broke the kiss.

"Yow!" she said. Her face was pure delight. "That's really fun."

"Oh, Kalma," Billy said. "I think I love you. I mean, Kalma, I mean, you're so lovely. I want to be with you."

Kalma sat back and Billy fretted. He assumed it was all over.

"We should be naked," she said, at last.

"We really should," Billy Kos said.

"Do you want to do it in my bedroom?"

"Yes," Billy Kos said.

She rose and took his hand (she's taking my hand, Billy's heart sang) and led him to the bedroom. The bedroom floor's detritus was not quite as thick but the bed was covered with schoolbooks and papers. Kalma let go his hand and bent over, sweeping everything onto the floor. Billy watched her backside as if it were the greatest show on Earth. The light from the living room was quite bright coming through the doorway.

"Ok," Kalma said. Billy thought she was going to brush her hands together as if they were ready to start work. "Oh, wait," she said. "Turn out the living room light please."

Billy was back in ten seconds. Kalma was under the covers.

"Should I undress? I mean, are you undressed?" Billy said. Only Kalma's head was visible in the yellow glim. She wore half a smile.

"Yes," she said.

Billy hesitated. He pulled his briefs gingerly over his erection, which looked like a cannon jutting out from his fort. Kalma looked him up and down. She held her gaze at his middle for a long time.

"Uh huh," Kalma said.

"What?"

"You can get in bed now."

Billy jumped under the covers. Kalma lay on her back and Billy placed a hand over her stomach.

"If I push your belly button your legs will fall off," Billy said.

"Is that literally true, Billy Kos?" Kalma opened her eyes wide. A genuine tremor ran through her.

"No, Kalma. Not literally true."

"Good night, Billy Kos," Kalma said.

"I," Billy said. His heart sank. It was just a sleepover.

"Good night, Billy Kos," she repeated, dreamily. "With the big dick."

And she slept.

## CHAPTER SEVEN

Coasta Kos was a young man when he and his wife, Bronwyn Kos (nee Hurston), adopted Billy from an orphanage in Brownsville, Tennessee. Coasta was 22 and had just started a job with Turner Dairy. Coasta was nostalgic for a time in the world that he never actually experienced, when milk was delivered to your door in glass bottles. Somewhere in his genetic memory he felt the thrill of chocolate milk, carried in cold glass, as a rare treat. He remembered his grandfather's tales of being a neighborhood milkman in what is now Midtown Memphis. Coasta was a 3rd generation Turner Dairy employee, though now his job was only clerical. Coasta also dressed like his grandfather in a neat gray suit, white shirt and thin dark tie.

Billy Kos loved his father with the kind of devotion that lost lambs must feel for the shepherd who finds them. Billy knew he was adopted but the word meant nothing to him. He could remember nothing before Coasta and Bronwyn's home. When Bronwyn died at thirty-seven Billy found himself consoling his father who was turned inside out by grief. He would never be the same again, and now that Billy and he lived alone, Billy often did the parental duties around the house while his father sat in his chair and sighed, or read romance novels (he had a special affinity for Rosemary Rogers and for the x-rated sagas of Zoey Nixon), or watched the rom-coms of Billy Crystal, Meg Ryan, and Cath Gallagher.

Billy cooked and cleaned and never complained. His father still worked his 8-hour days at the dairy, Monday to Friday, and Billy rarely missed a day of preparing dinner and having it ready when Coasta returned home. On weekends, they often ordered food to-go, or caught a ballgame at crumbling Autozone Park, where they supped on ballpark franks and popcorn. But, this week, Billy felt guilty for not making his father dinner on the two nights he took Kalma out.

"Billy," Coasta said, that evening at the dinner table (seared chicken livers, couscous and butter beans), "you have a new way about you. And I see you didn't sleep in your bed last night. What's going on, son?"

"Dad," Billy said, in a grave tone, "I've fallen in love."

Coasta was quiet a moment, wistful. His sigh was twice as deep, carrying the sigh also of his deceased wife. He smiled a reflective smile.

"Well, that's fine, son. Seriously fine. Who is the lucky female?"

"Her name is Kalma, Pops, and she is the prettiest woman at the University of Memphis. She is freckled head to toe and has legs that Taylor Swift would be jealous of."

"Head to toe, you say?"

Billy blushed and smiled at his plate. He lifted his head and when he did he saw his father smiling, also. His heart expanded.

"Father, I slept with her." Billy felt very mature saying it.

"Grand, Son, grand. You used a safe, I assume."

Billy was caught in his half-lie and knew no way out but ahead.

"Yes, Father. Always." This had the right tone, too.

"Very good, I knew you were my smart boy. Say, I believe one of the satellite stations is showing *You've Got Mail* tonight, if you'd care to join me."

Billy let a few beats pass. He did not think it right to remind his father that he had a digital copy in his film library. He speared a butter bean and held it up in front of his face.

"I believe I will be with my lady tonight," Billy Kos said. "But I can cancel if you'd like the company."

"Of course not, no, no. You go out. You do your homework?"

Now Billy's new maturity tottered.

"Yes. Or I will. Don't worry."

"Never worry about you, Billy."

They sat in peaceful silence and ate.

Then Coasta said, "Bring that young woman around soon."

"I will, Pops. She's dying to meet you."

## CHAPTER EIGHT

That night, since they had not gone out to eat, Billy and Kalma went to the movies at the once grand Malco Paradiso. They saw the new Allie Parmenter film, *A Small Bowl of Cereal.* Billy was unsure about the choice of movies since it was subtitled. Kalma ate popcorn like a child, in big fistfuls, and there was little opportunity for holding hands. Occasionally Billy would rest his palm on her thigh, which was clad in some stretchy manmade material, orlon or Teflon, and the small muscle in her thigh had a heartbeat like a bird's. Billy was happy.

On the drive back to Kalma's Billy returned his hand to the birdlike heartbeat.

"How did you like the film?" he asked.

"Hmm, mmm, I liked it," Kalma said, in her singsong cadence.

"Could you follow the subtitles ok? I didn't know it was in Spanish," he said. With celerity he added, "Some people don't like subtitles."

"Oh, yes, hmm, hmm. Some of the subtitles were badly translated."

Billy had to think about this for a minute.

"You speak Spanish?"

"The more difficult words were actually Basque."

"You speak Spanish?"

Kalma looked over at her date and smiled a little kitten smile.

When they got to Kalma's she fixed them some ice tea with Kool-Aid in it. They sat again on the ghastly couch. Billy thought, perhaps, just a bit, the room had been straightened. Some of the crustier food items had disappeared.

"Black tea and raspberry Kool-Aid," Kalma said, presenting it to Billy as if it were a fine wine.

"Mm, very good," polite Mr. Kos said. He couldn't wait to stop drinking it and start kissing Kalma. He swallowed a large amount, looked for a place to set the glass, settled on the floor at his feet, and put his hand to Kalma's dappled cheek.

"You look lovely tonight," he told her.

Kalma's cheek swelled with an intake of tea. She smiled and a tiny rivulet dribbled from the corner of her mouth.

"Your legs are so beautiful," he tried again.

"You told me," she said.

Billy put down his hand. He used the other hand to hold it in his lap as if it were a stubborn puppy.

"As soon as I finish this tea we can kiss," Kalma said.

Billy's smile was a suckling's.

Their mouths met hungrily and, again, Billy was astonished at how full and wet her lips were. He imagined them all over his body and his erection grew. He ran his hands along Kalma's bony ribcage and over her breasts. Her little nipples were as hard as cherry pits and she sighed into Billy's mouth as his fingers tweaked them.

When they broke the kiss, Billy said in a gush of emotion, "Oh, Kalma, I do love being with you. I am so happy right now right here."

Kalma giggled.

"Are you happy, Kalma?" Billy hated himself for asking.

"You're hard again," she said, nodding toward his lap.

"Of course I am," he replied.

"Just from kissing and nipple play," she said, matter-of-factly.

"Yes. I have such lust for you, Kalma."

"Hmm, hmm," she sang again.

"Should we go to the bed again?" Billy asked. His throat caught.

"Oho, Bucko. I have school tomorrow."

Billy thought this was nonsense. They both had school tomorrow.

"Nonsense," Billy said. "I have school tomorrow, too."

"Billy Kos. I have to study."

Billy's face looked like a paper bag after it had been used and crumpled. He felt he might cry but fought it.

"How about tomorrow, being Friday, I cook for you? Yes? I will make us dinner and then we can make out some more."

Could Billy wait 24 hours? He felt destitute. 24 hours was a lifetime. What if she found someone else before then? What if she died? What if he died? He would die a virgin, well not technically a virgin, but without ever having fucked a woman he loved.

"Ok," he said.

"Billy Kos, don't make with the sad song. Is it the erection? Does that hurt?"

Billy saw his chance. "A bit," he said.

"Hmm, hmm. Ok," Kalma said.

"What?" Billy was perplexed.

"You can kiss me some more and play with my nipples."

"How will that?"

"After then you can masturbate in the car going home. Boys do that. They really do."

Kalma seemed to want to impress her knowledge of such things on Billy. It was a crap deal—and Billy thought things had gone backwards—but he began to kiss her again anyway. Once again Kalma sighed—involuntarily?—when he tweaked her nipple so he moved a hand underneath her top and dug underneath the tight wired bra, and found the nipple with his fingers. Bare it felt like something almost electric.

"Ah, ah," Kalma said, breaking the kiss.

"Do you want me to stop?" Billy asked.

"More. No, do more."

Emboldened, Billy pulled up her top and pushed the bra up around her neck and began to roll her nipples between the fingers of both his hands. Kalma squirmed a bit and Billy moved his mouth to the left nipple. He sucked there and was as happy as a buttercup.

"Oh, oh, that's nice, Billy Kos. Yes, do that some more."

Billy moved a hand down her stomach and attempted to unsnap her skirt.

"Oops," Kalma said, falling back like a bag of grain. "Time to study. Time for you to take care of Mr. Magic."

She put a finger on the tip of Billy's erection through his jeans.

"Goodnight, Billy Kos," she said, kissing him on the nose.

One the way home the radio was playing "Fire," by Arthur Brown. Billy's wanker was in his hand. He was fantasizing about tomorrow night when he ran, jarringly, into a ditch.

## CHAPTER NINE

"I don't understand," Willie Waugh was saying. "You slept with her but you never put it in?"

"Willie, it's not like that. It was—*tender*. The moonlight shown on her skin."

He made up this last part but it seemed true to him. It seemed emblematic of what he was trying to say.

"You sure you want me to meet her?"

"I am not sure of that at all. But she is waiting for me in the student center and I told her you were with me."

"Ok, man. I'll try to turn my charm to low boil."

"Yeah, you do that."

In the lounge of the student center Billy spotted her from a hundred yards away. She was slumped down on a couch, one hand was pulling her lower lip, the other hand was picking her nose. She seemed to have no clue she was out in public. The back of her neck was almost level with the couch cushions and her legs, under a tennis skirt, were spread wide open. Today's color was a deep purple.

"Jesus," Billy said under his breath.

"You see her?" Willie said.

"Yeah, maybe today is not a good day."

"Aw, Buddy. I'm here. I'm ready. I'm charmless."

"I know, but I am not feeling good about this."

"You think I'm an asshole. You think I won't act like an adult."

"No, Willie, it's not that."

"What then? What?"

"I just—I don't know. Maybe after this weekend when I will know better if I really have a girlfriend or not—"

"Hey, look at that," Willie dug an elbow into Billy's side. "Beaver shot! Ha ha. She looks kinda simple. Ha ha. She's oblivious. But, damn, look at her fine legs."

Billy froze. His guts churned. He was looking at the floor and he was clenching and unclenching one hand.

"Billy—I said—" and Willie stopped. "Uh oh."

"Yes, that's the love of my life. The simpleton with the wide-open beaver."

"Shit, Billy, I'm sorry. Really. She's—she's quite pretty."

"Let's get out of here."

"Uh, Billy, she's waving at us."

"Shit."

Billy walked solemnly toward Kalma and Willie followed after. Kalma was sitting up now and looked more presentable.

"Hi Kalma," Billy said when they were ten feet away. "This is my friend Willie." He was rushing his speech. He wanted to be elsewhere. He wanted to be in Asia. Or on another planet. He would never live down this moment. His girlfriend was an idiot and his best friend saw it and judged him.

"Hello, Willie," Kalma said, and put out her hand. Willie took it. He almost bent to kiss it.

"Hi Kalma. Billy talks about you like you're a cross between Brigit Bardot and Iris Murdoch."

"I don't know who Iris Murdoch is," Kalma said.

"Novelist from way back," Willie said. "Wayback, Arkansas, I think."

Kalma saw the joke. She looked from face to face. And then the laugh spilled out like a slot machine paying off.

Billy watched her laugh and his smile widened. He glanced at Willie and saw that he was charmed by the laugh, also. It was Kalma's superpower.

The three ended up having lunch together and the coze was chummy and Kalma only seemed odd when she put mayonnaise on her French fries. Willie, if he noticed, did not comment. He was too busy making her laugh with stories of when he and Billy were young. Billy was happy again. Kalma even took his hand a few times on top of the table, holding it with her special warmth, a warmth that Billy was just recognizing but had not yet come to count on. And, at the end of the lunch, Kalma took his hand again.

"I've got to run to Chemistry. Nice to meet you, Willie. And, Boyfriend, I will see you tonight. Remember I'm cooking." And she kissed him a slightly wet kiss.

"She's dynamite," Willie said.

"I know," Billy replied. "I really know."

## CHAPTER TEN

"Pops, I put your dinner on the counter, ok?"

Billy had pan friend a pork chop and surrounded it with brown rice and peas. It made him hungry cooking it and he began to look forward to seeing Kalma for both his appetites.

"Well, that looks right tasty, Son," Coasta said, entering, tucking his shirt in. He always wore his work clothes until he took them off to replace them with pajamas. "You're going to see your paramour, right?"

"She's cooking me dinner for the first time."

"That's a good thing. Your mother was a marvelous cook," Coasta said. His voice got thick. He looked out the window, turning his head away from Billy's gaze. Billy was remembering his mother's cooking, which was so high in sodium it was surprising his blood still flowed.

"Yep, I gotta run now," Billy said, putting a hand on his father's shoulder.

"This is—how many? nights in a row with this new girl, ain't it son?"

"Four—five, I think," Billy said.

"That's the way it should be. When it's right it's right. After your mother and I went out for the first time a day didn't go by that we did not see each other. Not one day."

"I know Pops. That's the way. That's what I want in my life."

"You ever read Pogo, Billy?"

"Pogo, Pops?"

"The comic strip. Funny stuff. They don't have Pogo anymore."

"Ok, Pops. I might or might not be home tonight. I have no way of knowing."

"No," Coasta Kos said, his gaze wandering back to the great outdoors. It seemed to travel to the stars and take in the whole cerulean firmament. "We have no way of knowing."

As Billy's fist struck the door Kalma opened it. She was wearing a t-shirt, jean cutoffs and an apron. It was the first apron Billy had seen since his mom had worn one. It caught in his throat. Kalma was also holding a wooden spoon.

"Hello, Billy Kos," Kalma said, a smile teasing the corner of her mouth.

Billy stepped in and kissed her. Kalma threw her arms around Billy's neck and gave him a deeper kiss than expected. Billy was in paradise.

"Oops," Kalma said, stepping back. "I think you have orange sauce on your shirt now."

Billy tried to look over his own shoulder which made Kalma laugh her big brass laugh. Now Billy laughed.

"I can't see it," he said, inanely. "Orange sauce?"

"You know with tomatoes."

"Oh yes. It smells good. What is it?"

"Billy Kos you can't smell anything cuz it's not cooking yet. Lasagna."

"I fucking love lasagna," Billy Kos said.

"I love fucking—lasagna," Kalma said, and then laughed again at herself. Billy laughed too, stepping in and closing the door. Now he pulled her to him again and again their kiss was delightful.

"Gotta cook, Bucko. Set your butt down and watch TV till it's ready."

Billy saw the TV for the first time. Perhaps previously it had been covered in flotsam and jetsam, obscured by rubbishes. It was a black and white set with bunny ears. Yet, it was on and the picture was quite clear. Since the television stations had become property of the state the shows tended to be all re-runs. Right now *Twilight Zone* was on, the episode with the hitchhiker who keeps telling Inger Stevens, "I think you're going my way." Billy had seen it a thousand times. TV was mostly re-runs now, or soap operas. New shows were controlled by the government and that meant they were bland and upbeat.

From the kitchen came a din of pans beaten and dropped, of wooden spoons hitting metal in atonal composition, of refrigerator and oven doors opening and closing, and of Kalma doing her little Pooh-bear hums. Billy felt a king in a new kingdom.

"Drink?" Kalma called.

"Yes please."

"Come get it."

"Oh, yes," Billy said, rising.

The kitchen looked like a war zone with innumerable casualties. However, in the middle of the counter sat a lasagna which Kalma was just finishing by sprinkling orange cheese crumbles on top. The oven door stood open, ready to receive its task, making the kitchen a sweltering swamp.

"That looks delicious," Billy said.

"Just gonna pop it in," Kalma said, wiping her cheek and adding a broad red Native American swatch there.

"What kind of cheese is that you just sprinkled on top?"

"American. I just crumbled up the slices."

"Oh, I see. Unique."

"There's more American inside," Kalma said with pride.

"It looks well—layered," Billy said, stupidly. "You know, thick and tasty."

"Sloppy Joe in the middle, too," Kalma added. "I didn't have ground beef. But I also put some cloves of garlic in there and some cocktail onions. Sound good?"

"Uh huh," Billy said.

"Drinks in the fridge."

Billy opened the door. There were two pitchers.

"Which?" Billy said, straightening up.

"One is pure grape and the other is 3 flavors. I can't remember which. And there's ice tea but it's still dry. In the cabinet."

"Grape, I think," Billy said.

There was no dinner table and there were no TV trays, so they ate with plates in their laps. Now the TV was showing the *Green Acres* episode where Ralph Monroe falls for Hank Kimball, County Agent.

"I love this one," Kalma said. She was smiling like a toddler.

The lasagna was an adventure. It came from an imaginary Italy, where they use canned Sloppy Joe for their meat sauce. Billy managed to eat his whole plate.

Kalma was laughing at the television. Billy's heart, even heavy with undigested food, engaged. Kalma took her first bite ten minutes into the show.

"Yuck," she said. "This isn't very good. I don't know what went wrong. Usually I'm a pretty good cook. Hmm, hmm."

"It's very nice," Billy said, gallantly.

"You're nutsy. Something is off. I got a flavorsome dessert though."

She was gone before Billy could reply. She took both plates and they landed in the sink with a clatter and a crash. She returned, skipped twice, and landed beside Billy. She slung her legs (O those legs!) over Billy's lap. In each hand she held an orange Push-up.

"Push-ups," Billy said. "You read my mind."

As they sucked on the orange ice cream, and Kalma laughed at the worst jokes in Hooterville, Billy stroked those magnificent thighs. They were slightly parted and Billy was playing a game, seeing how close he could come to her crotch before Kalma reacted. When she finished her Push-up and tossed the soggy carton aside as if it were a champagne glass she still kept her attention locked on the television. As the show neared its inane conclusion Kalma laughed particularly loudly at one bit and right then Billy's fingers found themselves a sliver underneath the hem of her cutoffs.

"Woo!" Kalma said.

Billy froze but did not move his fingers.

"They are so funny," she said. She threw her head back onto the corner of the couch as if her laughter had exhausted her. "And your hand is making me tickly between the legs."

Billy unsnapped her shorts and began to tug them off her legs. He was momentarily entangled on her sandals but soon had them all the way off. Her panties were yellow. *The* yellow panties. Kalma had closed her eyes and her face had gone into mask mode. Billy ran a hand slowly from ankle to thigh. As he neared motherland Kalma parted her legs slightly. She wanted it! Billy almost swooned. He tried to concentrate. He knew he would remember this moment for the rest of his life.

First, he cupped his hand over her panties. He could feel her bush, spiky and dense, through the material. He kneaded it and was rewarded by an intake of breath. And then a dampness that smelled slightly of the woods. He increased the pressure. Did he know what he was doing? No, he was flying by the, well, the seat of his pants. And inside his pants his own desire was making itself urgently known.

He managed to work one finger inside the side of her panties and he felt how warm and wet she was. Now Kalma began to make little animal pants, expiration marks. "Heh, heh, heh. . ."

Billy took the yellow panties in his hands and lowered them, this time much quicker. Kalma lifted her rear end to aid him and once off she spread her legs wide. Billy was staring at Elysian Fields. It was dark and glistened like a grassland at night. He put a finger inside her and wiggled it around. She bucked upward. He put two fingers inside and she bucked upward again.

"Heh heh heh," she continued.

Billy ran one hand under the t-shirt and was surprised to find no bra. She had thought ahead. Again, he exhorted himself, she wants this. And, as he thought this, Kalma, without opening her eyes grabbed the hem of her shirt in two hands and pulled it over her head. She was spread out before him completely naked, a banquet. This was better than the surreptitious sneaking glances he stole in bed. She wanted him to see her, to take her.

Billy did not know how to take her. He knew he was expected to go down on a woman if he wanted oral sex in return, and God knows he did. He knelt on the floor. One knee fell on something crispy. Kalma opened her eyes, reassured herself that he was still there, and closed them again.

Billy put a hand on each thigh and Kalma opened her legs even wider. Billy put his tongue into the tangle of bush.

"Yipes!" Kalma said. Then: "Heh heh heh. . ."

Billy used his tongue and his fingers. He was fumbling around. He did not know what to do but everything he did brought spasms from Kalma. He found that his tongue high in her pubes and one finger inside her seemed to be delighting her best so he concentrated there.

"Oh Billy," he thought she said. She was whispering now. And then, suddenly, she tensed her body. Billy could feel the hard knots of muscle in her thighs. He pressed downward with his mouth. It was instinctual and, apparently, the right thing to do.

"FUCKING CHRIST!" Kalma yelled. She actually yelled. And her body shook for a few minutes. It seemed like a long time. Then she dropped and went limp, eyes still closed, a little kitty cat smile on her face.

Billy got back up on the couch and gently stroked her thighs and her wet crotch as he gazed at her beauty. Her nipples, he now saw in better light, were purple like eggplant. Eventually Kalma opened her eyes. She opened them exaggeratedly wide like a cartoon character.

"Whoopie!" she said.

"Oh Kalma," Billy said. He thought he was going to cry.

"Billy Kos. Little Billy Kos."

"My Kalma," Billy said, with a catch.

"My Billy," she returned, dreamily.

"I love you, Kalma."

Now she fixed him with her stare. With a half-smile she studied his face. She noted the glisten around his mouth, water from her well. Then she closed her eyes and said, very quietly, "I love you, too, Billy Kos."

Billy stripped off his clothes down to his underwear and put his hand out. Together they went to the bedroom. Billy didn't know whether to remove his briefs or not. Were they going to actually have intercourse? He had a 'safe,' as his dad called it, in his pocket and his pocket was on his pants and his pants were in the living room.

He lay down next to her and this time she returned his embrace. They kissed for a long time. At one point Kalma's hand went down Billy's stomach and teased the elastic band of his underwear. Billy subtly pushed his crotch upward in what he thought was an invitation. But the hand ascended again.

"Hmm, hmm," Kalma began.

"Kalma, you're beautiful. I could just look at your forever."

"Hey, Billy Kos. Do you want to see my ass? You've never seen my ass, have you? Huh? Tell me about my ass, Billy Kos."

She flipped over, dramatically.

Her ass was the perfect launching pad for her sempiternal legs. He began to pet it and, as he did, Kalma began humming again, and raising her ass up and down.

"Magnificent," Billy said, softly.

"My Billy," Kalma whispered back.

Billy stroked and stroked, petted and petted. Kalma rose and fell, rose and fell.

Then Billy's hand went back between her legs. A finger went inside her. Now Kalma pushed her ass against Billy's wrist.

"Whooosshhh!" she said quickly, and her body tensed again.

She fell back down. Billy removed his finger but continued to pet her ass.

"I had two orgasms," Kalma said. "Two whole orgasms."

"I thought so," Billy said.

"Hmm, hmm, my Billy Kos. Hmm, hmm."

"My Kalma," Billy said absently. His brain was on overload. He was trying to cling to the moment and it was slipping into history too quickly.

"And Billy Kos has none," Kalma said, in her childish singsong.

She flipped back over.

"Billy Kos," she said. "Show me your dick again please."

Billy laughed so Kalma laughed.

"Because I said dick?" she asked.

"No, no. Just so—formal."

"If you don't—"

Billy pulled his briefs off quickly. He flopped back beside her. And it was quite an erection, stiff, long, full of lifeblood.

Kalma leaned on one elbow and looked at it.

"Hmm, Billy's dick. Billy's dick is big. It's a big dick."

"Oh Kalma." Billy's emotions were running high.

"Billy Kos, lemme tell you something."

Billy waited. Finally he said, "What?"

"I don't know what to do."

"Oh," Billy said. "Oh, I see."

"Show me please."

Billy hesitated then began to pump himself a bit while Kalma watched.

"I like watching you. Would that be enough?"

"No," Billy said. Was this born of frustration or just an awkward answer?

"Okay, Billy Kos."

Kalma put a finger on the head. She pushed it the way one might the head of a Weeble. The room was partially lit from the living room but the bedroom door was half-closed. In the semi-dark Billy wondered if she could see well enough to understand what he had done.

"Wrap your hand around it," he coached.

She did. Billy sighed. He wanted to watch. It was beautiful, her long, freckled fingers stroking him.

"Smoother," Billy said.

"Yes, Billy Kos."

She found a rhythm. "Ooh," she said. "I like doing this."

"I—huh—like it too."

"It's gonna get you off, isn't it?"

"It might—huh—my love."

She kept going, watching herself, watching his response.

"I—huh—want to make love with you, Kalma. I—huh—love you so much."

Kalma stopped. She removed her hand and laid it softly on Billy's chest.

"I don't know," she said. "I don't know, Billy Kos."

"We don't have to tonight." He sounded reasonable to himself. Kalma wore a puzzled moue.

"Do you want to come in my mouth instead?"

Billy almost laughed. His mind was on fire. He couldn't think. He couldn't make speech.

"Yes, m-my love," he managed.

Now, on her knees, her beautiful backside half-lit, Kalma began to work him with her hand and she placed her mouth over Billy's swollen head. She looked like a snake charmer trying to make the jism come out of the basket. Billy was still watching. Those thick wet lips. He wanted them on him. Kalma seemed determined to take his come without sucking him.

He chanced moving his hips upward slightly. She moved back slightly.

He pushed further. The head went in her mouth. Her hand hesitated. Then she began to pump him slowly and her incredible lips closed softly around his head. Then, bit by bit, her mouth went further down until she had to move her hand. Not having anything to do with it she wrapped it around Billy's scrotum.

When Billy came Kalma held on. She took it all. Billy shot off straight down her throat. After he was done she was still frozen on him, her mouth covering his entire cock. Then she pulled off, with an audible pop sound that she made for fun. And an exaggerated swallowing noise to follow.

"Ta-da!" she said. "Gulp, gulp, gulp."

Billy couldn't talk. His body was still twitching. Little bits of come still slipped from his cock. He almost passed out.

"Billy Kos, Billy Kos, are you in there?" Kalma was poking his forehead with her forefinger.

"Kalma Voyles, I will love you until I die," Billy said. And then he opened his eyes.

"I gave you a blowjob!" she crowed.

"Yes, Love."

"It was a good blowjob, too. I could tell. It was really good!"

"It was my love. You do everything well."

She lay her head on his chest.

"Do I, Billy Kos? I—I don't think so sometimes."

Billy held her. He stroked her hair. And sometime in the next half-hour they each fell asleep, naked, cradled, satisfied: lovers.

## CHAPTER ELEVEN

They began to spend every night together. Billy checked with his dad and his dad, bless him, gave his sanction. The oral sex lessons for both of them deepened. They became adept. But intercourse was still not on the menu.

One school day they met for lunch in the cafeteria. Billy asked Willie not to attend. Willie pretended his nose was out of joint.

"Are you putting mayonnaise on your French fries?" Kalma asked, her eyes wide with wonder.

"I am," Billy Kos said. "I am easily influenced."

"I influence you." She said it as if now she knew it to be fact.

"What classes did you have this morning? I was operating on no sleep," Billy said.

"Oh classes. You know, *science*."

"Are your grades ok? I'm not making it hard for you to pass?"

Billy half-hoped he was.

"Hmm, hmm, grades," Kalma said. She put half a Hostess Twinkie in her mouth.

"I'm sorry. We're not gonna compare grades or anything. Listen, I understand, I am holding onto this B average like grim death."

"Billy Kos, I'm a straight A student."

She put the other half of the Twinkie in her mouth. Billy was speechless. They ate.

"It's easy, that's all," Kalma elaborated.

"How are you paying for school? You have no part-time job?"

"Billy, my father, you know."

"I assure you I don't." Billy had an edge to his voice he did not remember honing.

"He's Voyles, of Voyles Chemicals."

"Voyles Chemicals," Billy parroted like a parrot.

"What does your dad do? You don't have a part-time job," Kalma said.

"I did. I used to. But I quit to concentrate on senior year and make sure I graduate. I was working at FedEx Wrestling Arena. Sweeping up and stuff. Dad had some savings and I'm using that to finish up."

After the Trump kakistocracy, after he wrote into law that all sports teams must have over 50% white athletes, many of the major franchises collapsed. The Memphis Grizzlies of the NBA was one victim, and the Forum, where they used to play, was turned into a wrestling arena and museum. It was more popular than the Grizzlies had ever been and many blacks moved away from Memphis. Many left the country.

"You're rich," Billy said, in wonder. "And brilliant."

"And pretty," Kalma added.

"Beautiful," Billy said.

"Hmm, hmm. I hate money. Hey, Billy Kos, remember last night, that thing you did. You know, with your finger and me bum?"

"Oh Kalma. Yes. It was a good experiment, wasn't it?"

"It was Billy Kos. I had a big old orgasm. When can we do it again?"

"Tonight, my love," Billy was talking in a dream.

"I kinda want it now if you have time."

And that is how they were caught in the women's bathroom with their pants down. There were crazy bathroom laws at this time but the school janitor did not turn them in. Billy didn't know his silence was bought by a little donation Kalma made to the janitor's family fund.

## CHAPTER TWELVE

> Later on, feeling expended, he lay again in kindness gently rooting in soft clefts, rocking and drifting on smoothness, afloat and basking in softness. He clasped a waist, his penis nestled between two gentle mounds and he was filled with kind nowhere.
>
> —Alasdair Gray

Billy Kos and Kalma Voyles first had intercourse at Billy's house in the bed he had slept in since a child. Coasta was out of town and the lovers enjoyed a carefree weekend there. They were both quite thrilled to finally do it and when Billy came inside Kalma he remembered the safe in his wallet. Too late.

He decided not to mention it to her. It went like this:

"These hot dogs are especially good," Kalma said. She kept looking at the interior of the wiener after every bite.

"I think they have some beef in them," Billy said.

"Oh. What's for dessert?"

"I think I bought Dad some Ding-Dongs. There might be some left."

Since the collapse of the health food industry almost everyone ate packaged food from the major food corporations.

"My dad has a color TV."

"Really? Color?" Kalma had to put down her hotdog and wipe her mouth.

"Yes, and many recorded shows."

So, after a dessert of Poptarts (Coasta had indeed eaten all the Ding-Dongs but he had left the package in the pantry with crumbs in it) they repaired to the paneled den and turned on the television. Billy began looking through the film library.

"Oh look! *Honey West*! In color!" Kalma exclaimed.

"Would you rather watch that?"

"Yes, please."

After a few minutes Billy was bored but Kalma was rapt like a child at the Annunciation. Billy idly ran a finger up and down her thigh, which was bare. Now she almost exclusively wore short dresses because she knew it pleased Billy.

At the commercial break, an ad for the brand-new assault rifles, Kalma turned to Billy and put her generous mouth onto his. They kissed until the show re-began.

After *Honey West* Kalma asked what they had recorded.

"Lots of westerns," Billy said. "Dad loves his oaters. And, um, Jerry Lewis."

"I love Jerry Lewis," Kalma said, seriously.

"And some porn."

During the Trump presidency porn had been elevated to acceptable home entertainment and pornographic videos and channels were as easy to get as soda pop.

"I've never seen porn."

"Well, Kalma we can do that if you'd like." Billy's hands were sweating. He actually had not watched a lot of porn himself.

He put a cartridge in the player. It contained 30 full-length triple-x movies.

The list of titles made Kalma giggle. "Lots to choose from," she said.

"How about *Ranch Nymphos*?"

"Ok. Ranch like the dressing."

Billy looked at Kalma to see if she were joking. She smiled wide so he laughed.

The movie didn't take long to get down to business.

"Oh," Kalma said. She sat forward.

Billy put a hand on her back. "We can stop this whenever you say."

"Shh." Kalma was paying attention to the dialog. She may have been the first human being to do that during an adult movie.

"Wow," she said, at one point.

Billy's erection jittered.

"Look at that," Kalma said. She was speaking to herself, Billy thought, as if he weren't there.

After 45 minutes, she leaned back. "Ok," she said.

Billy turned the television off.

"Ok?" he asked.

"Hmm, hmm," she said. "Billy Kos, Billy Kos."

Billy waited. He was accustomed now to the ragged rhythms of their conversations.

"I didn't know you could do that," Kalma said.

"What's that, Love?"

"You know. Where the woman was leaning over."

"From behind?"

"Yes."

"I suppose one can. I mean, two can."

Kalma giggled. Then, like a kettle coming to boil, the giggles gradually grew into whoops of laughter. "Oh my God," she kept saying.

Billy had to laugh, too, though he knew not at what. After a few minutes, she ran down.

"Billy Kos, do you want to do that with me?"

"From behind, you mean?"

"Well, maybe eventually. I mean, putting your dick inside me."

"You know I do, Love. When you are ready."

"Let's do it tonight then."

"Oh yes," Billy said.

So, they arrived bedside in Billy's childhood bedroom. Billy took her in his arms and their kiss was warm and affectionate.

They undressed each other slowly. Right down to the skin. And they held each other again, kissing and whispering endearments. Each knew that this was momentous. They hung Kalma's midnight blue panties over the bedside lamp.

"Nicely nice," Kalma said. "Dark blue light."

Once supine Billy found her with his fingers and she wrapped her soft hand around him. This was their usual preliminary activity. But, instead of oral sex they now contemplated making carnal congress for the first time.

"How should we do it?" Kalma asked Billy as if he were the expert.

"I don't know," Billy said. He was nervous. "Do you want to get on top of me?"

"Sitting on your dick? Facing you?"

"Yes, I suppose so."

So, she did. She climbed aboard and Billy helped steer the head outside her wet opening. At first Kalma's expression was cockeyed, as if she doubted this was right. Then she brightened.

"Here we go!" Kalma said.

He slid in easily. There was no resistance. It was as if they were yin and yang. Kalma's vaginal walls hugged Billy tightly. Billy was turned on by his woman's squinched up face and her deep purple nipples. At first neither moved, neither seemed to know who should take control. Nature did. Kalma, as she got turned on, began to move in a way that allowed her maximum contact with Billy's central point. It was a slow sinuous dance, perfected down the eons, her sizeable rump seeming to contract and expand.

They did very well for their first time. Kalma came twice and after the second time she reached back and grabbed Billy's balls and squeezed. Billy burst inside her.

And then realized he had forgotten the rubber.

Kalma lay down on top of Billy, his semen running out of her like a minute runnel.

"Oh Billy. Just like in the soap operas."

Billy smiled and held her tight. He loved her with a passion almost extirpated from the foreshortened world.

"You fuck good," Kalma said, softly.

"Honey," Billy whispered back.

"You fuck good with your big dick." Kalma was practicing. Billy thought she wanted to use new terms. She wanted to speak like the actresses in the adult film. "I like your big dick in me. You fuck so sweet. You fuck so good. You fuck so hard. Fuck me, Fuck me with your big dick."

Billy squeezed her tight. He wondered, not for the first time, if his dick was really big.

In the morning, after they both slept like innocent babes, they fucked again, this time with Billy on top. Again, they did it without protection.

## CHAPTER THIRTEEN

After seeing each other every night for thirteen weeks Kalma asked Billy to move in with her. Billy's expression was a grab-bag of conflicting emotions. *What a dump*, prevailed. But, also this: Kalma naked, Kalma wearing only a towel, Kalma in lingerie. And, of course, he loved her like immortal death. His world was Kalma.

"That would be splendid, yes," Billy said.

"It only makes sense."

"It really does."

Billy had a hard time breaking it to his dad.

"Son, you're never here anyway. You spend every night at her house. It only makes sense."

People are so sensible, Billy thought.

"I can still come by and get your dinner every night," Billy said.

"Bill, I can feed myself," Coasta said. On rare occasions he called Billy Bill. Billy could never figure out if it was more affectionate or less. Like adding someone's last name when you're angry.

"Are you sure, Pops?"

"Billy, go to her."

Billy kissed his father's white, whiskery cheek. He looked like Popeye's Pappy.

"Just make sure you send me an invitation to your graduation. I can't remember the date."

"Pops, you've got the invitation. It's this Saturday. I can pick you up."

"Saturday, of course. I'll get a ride. Don't you worry. I can ride in with someone."

Billy worried about his father's vagueness.

Both Billy and Kalma were graduating on that day, at the FedEx Wrestling Arena. After graduation, Kalma already had a job teaching in the Psychology Department. She had graduated at the top of her class, 4.0, with a bullet. Billy had graduated in the middle of the pack and was daily searching the job boards for employment. Meanwhile, he was helping out at the dairy.

On Saturday Billy and Kalma drove together to the arena. They parked a few streets away and walked hand-in-hand, in their ceremonial robes, to the giant toadstool with seating for 50,000. In the halls they mingled with some other graduates. Willie was there, stoned as a boiled owl.

"Brother and Sister," he exclaimed throwing his arms open and embracing them both. "You look like an R-rated version of Handel and Gretel."

"Hansel," Billy said, grinning like a goat.

"What did you call me?" Willie said, sputtering with laughter. "Seriously y'all are too beautiful for this old ecosphere. You need to spawn, you know?"

"Hmm, hmm, Willie Waugh. Nutty Willie," Kalma said. She was looking around for her father. He owned part of FedEx Wrestling Arena and she assumed he would be backstage waiting for her.

Billy leaned closer to Willie and said, sotto voce, "We're moving in together."

Willie wrinkled his brow. "My place?"

"Not you and me, lunkhead. Kalma and I are moving into her place."

Willie wrinkled his brow. "Oh, wow. That's a great idea. A great idea. Is her place nice?"

Billy hesitated. "We'll make it so."

Willie smiled. "Ah, Love. The ultimate fixer-upper. This is a good thing, Billy. You don't want to end up like me, good job but living alone, lonely, as Flaubert said, as this little finger."

"Are you lonely, Buddy?"

"The only advantage I can see to living alone is that you can take a crap with the door open."

Willie delivered this with the utmost seriousness. Billy smiled.

"Dadsy!" Kalma called, exiting as quickly as a man pursued by a bear.

"Did she say, Dadsy?" Billy asked.

Billy and Willie watched as Kalma threw her arms around an outsized, distinguished gentleman who was wearing a bespoke suit of clothes too nice for this event. Billy made a shameful, silent prayer that his dad not now appear.

Kalma hung on her father's neck while the old guy nuzzled her bright hair and cast a glance over the embrace at the two friends. Billy wondered which of the two he would pick, if he could pick, for a son-in-law.

"Son-in-law?" Billy said to himself. "Oh my."

"Billy Kos, Billy Kos, this is my father," Kalma came swiftly toward them, the old fellow in tow. Kalma had him by the sleeve of his expensive suit. "Bobby Voyles."

"Hello, sir," Billy said, stepping forward. "I'm so glad to finally meet you."

"Are you, son?" the old fellow spoke.

Billy's heart closed, compressed like a fist. Then a sly smile spread on the pater's face and he warmly wrung Billy's hand. He had a grip like an orangutan. His black hair with Cesar Romero white streaks and his tanned, lined face gave him the mien of an old-time matinee idol. His eyes were light blue like Kalma's.

"I understand you and Kalma will be living together," he said now, with a twinkle.

"Yessir. If you approve," Billy said. Inside his head he hit himself with a hammer.

"I was led to believe that this was a forgone conclusion. Kal did not give me the ultimate yay or nay."

"Dadsy, stop it," Kalma said. She slapped his shoulder. Around her father Kalma seemed eleven years old.

"I'm Willie," Willie said, extending a hand darkened by roach burn.

"A friend of Billy's, I assume." Mr. Voyles shook Willie's hand quickly as if he believed the Zika virus was still around.

"I'm sorry. My best friend, Willie Waugh," Billy said.

"Nice to meet you, sir. Your daughter's a very lucky man."

It was then that the sea of gowned figures began moving in one direction.

"We're part of this herd," Willie said, walking away.

"Gotta go, Dadsy. Catch you after." Kalma kissed his immaculate cheek.

On the way in she returned her hand to Billy's and squeezed it gently. She seemed happy as a reprieved felon.

Billy remembered little of the ceremony. He was between two strangers, one a red-headed kid (he looked 16) with a gap in his teeth, who kept mumbling prayers, and the other a woman short and stout like Totie Fields. She smiled at him whenever he glanced at her and seemed about to speak when Billy turned his head.

When he crossed the stage there was not one whistle, shout or hurrah. Later, he lingered in the back and waited for Kalma to pick up her diploma and her summa cum laude recognition. As she mounted the stage Billy noticed that her gown had been tucked into her underwear in the back (she must have gone for a quick pee before the ceremony) and she was showing a nice gam and one shiny cheek. Someone yelled, "Nice ass!" and the audience cheered and laughed. Kalma stopped at the edge of the stage and shyly waved. She did not know she was popular.

Later they found each other in the hallway. Someone had clued her in by then and her gown was hanging freely.

"Congratulations, Brainiac," Billy said and gave her a 3-second kiss.

"I'm glad that's over. I was nervous but the applause was nice."

"Yes," Billy said. "You deserve it."

They walked outside into the cerulean day, the sky like an upturned bowl. Billy's cell phone rang. It was not a number he recognized.

"Hello?"

"Billy Kos?" a woman's voice said.

"Yes," Billy said. "Speaking."

"This is Pipkin Stacks with the Memphis Police Department."

"Y-yes," Billy said, his heart sinking. Where was his father?

"I have some bad news."

Billy waited. If he was supposed to respond he was not going to. He wanted his life to freeze here in this moment of dread.

"Your father, Billy. I'm afraid he's dead."

"He-he can't be," Billy said. Of course, he could be. And he was.

"An accident apparently. He turned the stove on to make himself dinner last night and the pilot light had blown out. Meanwhile, apparently, he took a nap on the couch. He never woke up. The smell of gas was pretty strong even this morning."

"I-I don't know. I don't know what to do next. What do I do next?"

Tears were slipping out of Billy's eyes. Kalma moved closer and put her arm around him and rested her head on his chest.

"Can you come home right now?" Pipkin Stacks said.

## CHAPTER FOURTEEN

Coasta Avril Kos's funeral was held on a Saturday. There was a graveyard service only. The minister, an aged actor named Tom Cruise, was from The Church of Scientology (the National Church as instigated by President Trump) and the gibberish he spoke did not even penetrate Billy's ears. Billy wept openly. Kalma stood by him, her hand squeezing his. She shed a tear or two herself.

"You never even met him," Billy sobbed in the car on the way to the wake at Billy's old house. "He would have loved you."

"I would have loved him too, Billy Kos," Kalma said.

The wake was sparsely attended. About ten guys from the dairy and their wives. Billy knew a few but not well. These co-workers provided the food. Billy mostly stood in one spot and shook hands and received kisses on his cheek from the lipsticked older ladies.

It turned out that besides the house Billy inherited his father's savings, which were still considerable, even after paying for Billy's last year in college. His dad had never spent money on himself.

This solved the problem the couple faced moving into Kalma's trashed apartment. And, when she moved into Coasta's house she had few possessions worth transferring to her new home. She left the apartment how it was and, of course, did not get her security deposit back.

The first night in the new house they rechristened Coasta's double bed with their coitus. In the days to come that room gradually became theirs, as Billy let go of each of his father's possessions, slowly, reluctantly.

They kept the furniture initially, until Bobby 'Boils' Voyles began sending over one expensive piece of furniture at a time. He had never visited their new home. He assumed the décor would be second rate; trouble was Boils' taste in furnishings was atrocious.

Not that it mattered to Billy or Kalma. Both were so involved with each other that little else penetrated. Billy penetrated, time and time again. Sex became part of their language, the special sociolect new lovers create, catch-phrases and footle, quotations and love-talk. They did it in every room, on every new and old piece of furniture. They did it standing, in the shower, in the kitchen, where Kalma accidentally turned on one burner of the stove, leaning over it, taking her lover's thrusts from behind.

"Yipes!" she said as a flame licked near her cheek. "Don't stop!"

She let the fire burn but moved a few inches to the right.

And in all this love-making, Billy pondered, there was no thought of protection. He thought they were dreaming, that they were irresponsible and nothing mattered but that they stay as close to each other as possible, hand-in-hand, cheek-to-jowl, yoni to yang.

## CHAPTER FIFTEEN

The work at the dairy was anathema to Billy. He did not fit in with the workers, some who knew his father, some who did not. The ones who did looked upon Billy as a poor chip off his father's honest, wholesome block. The ones who did not looked upon Billy as a smarty-pants (college graduate, they sniffed, in *anthropology*).

Billy longed to find different work. Casting about in his rackety-packety head he despaired of all the things he did not know how to do.

"Why not one of the new shops at the mall?" Kalma asked one night.

"Malls. How did they come back?"

"They left once upon a time?"

"I don't know. I've heard some of the old tales. What could I do in the mall? Sell women's blouses? Book virtual reality tours? Electronics? I don't know an aPhone from a ZipPhone. A to Z, I'm a dunce."

"Come here, baby," Kalma said. She put her arms around her mate. He rested there, succor, support, suspension. She held him and with one hand pulled down her lower lip.

"Hey, I'm teaching a graduate class now. Whee, these kids are smart. And beautiful. All the men look like Rockaday's lead singer."

"I don't know who Rockaday is," Billy pouted.

"You wanna get sushi?"

"Yes, I do. I do wanna get sushi," Billy said, smiling at his wife's lopsided conversational style.

"I'll order. You pick up."

Billy tried to counter Kalma's inherent disarray by being a good househusband. He spent a lot of time straightening, dusting, mopping, arranging. Sometimes he could not keep up with his wife's penchant for dropping wrappers on the floor and leaving clothes wherever she took them off. Billy did the laundry and the dishes, too. If not, they would sit for days. He experimented and it was so.

## CHAPTER SIXTEEN

It turned out Kalma Kos was a dynamite teacher, loved by both students and her peers. Among the faculty her favorites were Manila Zamboni, who taught in the English department, Ronnie 'Rev' Rollerton, head of the science department, and Black 'Red' Stendhal, who taught with Kalma in Psychology. Red, though married to the runway model, Theodora Backless, thought himself a lady's man and his flirtations were notorious, among faculty and students alike. (When they abolished the statutory rape law campuses across the country became a bit dicier for women to navigate.) It was said, though no one ever proved anything, that Red had fathered at least two children by his students, and one by Ms. Pulliam in the art department. Ms. Pulliam, for her part, preggers, seemed to glow and flow on campus, her womanlier figure quite alluring until she had to take a sabbatical and came back her usual slim, shapeless self. It was further said that the child has bright red hair and is being raised by Ms. Pulliam's mother, an ex-Marine.

Among the students Kalma was well-liked because she never minded spending time with them, often taking part in after-school activities like going for ice cream and shopping for second-hand clothes. She was also well-liked for sitting on her desk in front of the class with her legs open and her bright colored panties on display.

"Ms. Kos has the best legs on the campus, teacher or student," Jim Trippett said to the boys in the locker room.

"And the prettiest panties," his pal Rocket Calamari added, wistfully staring off into the high-ceilinged corners. "Ms. Kos," he added in a private whisper.

Kalma began to do things in the evenings, various school activities or dinners with Manila or the Stendhals. Billy felt slightly bereft. He missed his Kalma. Their sex life, which Billy had fantasized about until it took the form and shape of a grand myth, was intermittent. Sometimes they had wonderful sessions together. Sometimes Billy would watch his absent-minded wife cross the room clad only in panties and sneakers and then he'd go into the bathroom and masturbate. Billy wanted sex every night, and sometimes in the mornings, too. Kalma was not as needy and Billy was forced to wait for her mercurial moods to spin the wheel and land on sex.

Billy hated his job. And right about the time when he thought he couldn't take it anymore he found a new position at the library as manager of their digital books. Billy had no qualifications for the position and could only surmise that there were not many applicants, which was true since the library was underfunded (President Trump asked rhetorically in his state of the union address, "Government money, really, for free books? Sad.") and not very popular anymore.

"I got the job," Billy crowed into his phone.

"What job?" Kalma asked. She was having a drink with her student, Rocket Calamari, who had asked her to talk over his grades at the Illiterate Bar, the nearest watering hole to the campus.

"The library. I told you I was applying."

"Is that a schwa?"

"Schwa—what? Kalma are you listening to me? What are you doing?"

"It's not a schwa. It's an umlaut."

"Kalma!"

"Billy, are you still there? I understand now. You got the library job."

"I did, yes. And I quit the dairy right away."

"Ok," Kalma said.

"What are you doing? Kalma, where are you?"

"I'm helping a student with his handwriting. I mean his classwork."

"Handwriting? Who writes by hand anymore?"

"What, Billy?"

"Nothing. Never mind. Listen, let's celebrate tonight. Dinner at Folks Folly, what do you say?"

Kalma's laugh exploded into the phone. This time it did not tickle Billy.

"That's not even English!" Kalma roared.

"Kalma, come home. Come home soon and let's do dinner."

"What? Ok, Billy. I'll be there where you said."

She hung up.

Billy was steamed. He paced and kicked at articles of Kalma's clothing that were in odd places on the floor. One of her nylons (had he ever seen her in nylons?) was in front of the dishwasher in the kitchen. "Of all the—" Billy cussed her privately.

When she got home, over an hour later, Billy had mostly lost his anger. She came in smelling of drink but dressed to the nines, even the upper nines. She wore a white dress with large black and white polka dots and her bare legs ended in white socks inside saddle oxfords. Billy wanted her, not just in the bedroom, though there was always that, but in his life. He could never let her go, no matter how much she exasperated him.

"Is that what you were wearing when you left the house this morning?" he asked, his momentum arrested by her beautiful figure.

"Did you say shteaks?" Kalma said, with a strange leer. She was vamping?

"What? Yes. Steaks. At Folks Folly. To celebrate my new job."

"You got a new job? I'm so proud of you." She stepped toward him and bussed his cheek. He could smell the booze and underneath it her particular funk, sweat and sex. She had a musk.

"I told you on the phone. At the library. I'm going to be in charge of digital books." Billy beamed.

"Wonderful," Kalma answered, but a sleepiness had entered her voice.

"Do we need to make reservations?" Billy asked.

"I have no reservations," Kalma said and giggled. "I have no inhibitions either. Or institutions. Or watusis." She giggled some more.

"Kalma, we're going to eat at Folks Folly, ok? Are you ready already?"

"Ready already alrighty."

It was difficult to ascertain if this was tipsiness or Kalma's usual spaced-out speech. Not for the first time Billy wondered how she taught classes and was such an academic success.

In the car Kalma put her seat back a bit and stretched out. She smiled a sweet, closed-eye smile and deliberately pulled her dress up well over her thighs. Billy sighed, received a rude honk, and concentrated on the road for the rest of the trip to the restaurant.

Folks Folly was still a popular eatery. Since the eating of all kinds of animal flesh had taken on a new cachet their thick beef and buffalo steaks were much honored. There was a small table for two in the back room and that is where Billy and Kalma sat and ate their seared pulp.

"Mm, mm good," Kalma said, patting her belly in mock passion.

"They still do a dynamite piece of meat here," Billy said. He was faking it. He'd never eaten here before because he could not afford it. He wasn't sure he could now.

"Kalma, what were you doing this afternoon?" Billy asked, after the plates had been cleared and the crème brulee ordered.

"School, Billy Kos, I teach school."

"I mean after that. You know I mean after that."

"Conference with a student."

"Which student."

"Is that Stan Yumont?" She nodded her head toward a table across the room.

Billy looked. It did resemble the actor, son of the infamous leading man Dan Yumont.

"I think so," Billy said.

"I loved him in that remake of *It's a Wonderful Life*," Kalma said. Her eyes glistened.

"Yes, yes, he's quite good."

"Better than good, I'd say."

"Better than good. Though, strictly speaking, the film was not a remake and it was entitled *It's a Terrible Life*, turning the tables on the original. If you remember the glimpse of what the world would be like after the hero's death was a rosy picture. His life had only added negative aspects to the world."

Kalma had already mentally moved on.

"I love crème brulee," she said, smiling her wide, sloppy smile at the young waiter, who seemed nonplussed by the radiance.

"Kalma, so I think, with this new job and with your salary, and what's left of Dad's savings, we will be doing quite well," Billy said, swirling a spoon in his dessert, his heart beating too fast. He felt as if something were wrong but he couldn't grasp it.

"I'm well, thank you," Kalma said, and she put a dot of crème on the tip of Billy's nose with her spoon.

"Kalma, stop it!" Billy said. It came out more heated than he intended.

Kalma sat back. She opened her eyes wide. Her face was frozen momentarily. Then she slowly licked her lips and pulled on the ample bottom one.

"I'm sorry, Billy Kos," she said. "I'm sorry."

Billy felt like an ass. Yelling at Kalma was akin to pushing an overly affectionate puppy out of your lap.

"Kalma, no, I'm sorry," he said. But he had lost the thread if there had ever been a thread.

"Let's go home and make love," Kalma said, seriously.

"Make love," Billy repeated in a dreamy voice. "Make. Love."

'You know, fuck," Kalma said, taking Billy's hand.

"Marry me," Billy Kos said.

## CHAPTER SEVENTEEN

Billy and Kalma were married in an outdoor ceremony on the ground that used to be Brooks Art Museum. After the museum closed the area because a large grassy sward, originally intended as a parking lot for visitors to the zoo and its new Killer Orca section. But the zoo ran out of money and the campaign to raise funds petered out and so the area was now only a pretty field. Their wedding was not the first held there. Kalma had heard about it as a possible site from Ms. Pulliam, who used to volunteer at Brooks.

"It's lovely, from what I hear," Ms. Pulliam said. "I think there's a tree or two left standing."

But before the hymeneal ceremony something momentous and frightening had to occur: Billy had to visit Kalma Voyles' father's estate, Karenhaal. He had to have dinner with robustious Boils Voyles and his wife, Renata, nee Leatherman. Renata had been a beauty queen when young and had even gone to Hollywood for a screen test. But when she married Boils he forbade her having a job so she returned to Memphis and settled into her life of taking care of their baronial home, with its large staff, helped and hindered by her addiction to opioids.

The drive to the estate, which sat on about 25 acres in Old Raleigh (a small town which was once the county seat, then a part of Memphis, then its own municipality again after seceding from the big city in 2019), took about 45 minutes due to the sections of unfinished interstate and boulevards dug up years ago which had fallen victim of the Anti-Infrastructure Act, which ended road work in the whole country.

"It's gonna be great," Kalma said, on the drive over. "I think Kissy is frying up some chicken. You know the secret to southern fried chicken is a closely guarded secret among nigger women."

Billy would have winced at the n word, though it was back in vogue, if he were not paralyzed by fear.

They were met at the door by a darkie extra from *Gone with the Wind*.

"Tomboy," Kalma said, and leapt at the older black gentleman, kissing him on the lips for a very long time.

"Whew!" Kalma said, when the servant set her back down. "What a great kisser! Oh, and Tomboy, this is Billy Kos. He wants to marry me."

The home was like a movie set. One expected William Powell and Myrna Loy to appear, highballs in hand. The rooms were as large as the pastures of the sun and the furnishings dark and heavy. The foyer alone could have housed twenty street arabs. To the right was a dining room with a table King Arthur would have been happy to use for his copious repasts. The table was unset.

"Why isn't the dining room ready, Tomboy?" Kalma said, pausing in her giddiness.

"Mister V said y'all would be eating in the kitchen, Ms. Voyles."

Kalma looked at Tomboy. She looked at Billy. She pulled her lip.

Then she set off at a furious pace toward the kitchen.

"Should I follow her?" Billy asked.

Tomboy looked Billy up and down. "I'm guessing so."

Billy scampered after his fiancé. He found her around two sharp corners in the kitchen where there was a massive center table set for five, a fireplace blazing away, two black cooks, two black servants, and Boils Voyles. Kalma was nose to nose with her father. Their discussion was furious but muted. Billy only caught the occasional word. He also caught the eye of one of the serving women and she winked her soft brown eye. Did Billy know why? He did not.

"Willy!" Mr. Voyles roared.

"Billy, sir," Billy said, approaching the outstretched hand, which waited for him like an executioner.

"Bobby," Bobby Voyles said.

"I'm sorry?" Billy said, his hand now part of Boils Voyles' three-hand stack.

"No need to be sorry, son. Great to see you again. I understand you're the scapegrace that wants to marry my daughter."

"Yes. Yes, sir I do. Very much."

Just then Kalma's mother entered. She was around 55 with sharp lines carved into what was once a remarkable face. The beauty was still there though hardened like plaster. Her eyes were almost entirely sclera and seemed colorless like the eyes of an albino. Her body was compact, almost too thin, in contrast to her husband's healthy girth. Their sybaritic lifestyle was feeding him and starving her.

"Willy," she said, putting her hand out.

"Billy, ma'am," Billy said. His hand was taken, recently having vacated Boils' plump enclosure, between Renata's soft, ex-debutante hands and was cradled there as if it were a mouse. She looked Billy directly in the eye and held her gaze there until Billy had to look away. His eye fell to her mouth which was as full-lipped as her daughter's. He watched her mouth work its way slowly toward a smile. It was like watching craquelure beginning to peel.

"Dinner's ready, sir," Tomboy said, materializing at Mrs. Voyles' elbow, which he took and helped her to her seat at the table.

"Grand!" Boils Voyles thundered. His tanning bed tan seemed to move without him. It was shyer than the man it covered.

The fifth member of the table was Kalma's brother, Arch. He wore a timeless crewcut and what they used to call tennis whites when tennis was a popular sport, before the net shortage of 2021. Perhaps the Voyles still had courts. Perhaps that's the why of Arch's look.

"Hey, Bookman," Arch said, archly.

"I'm sorry. What?" Billy said. He was confused when he entered the house and his confusion was growing like a static electric cloud of anger.

"Aren't you the author?" Arch said, archly.

"He's a librarian, Dopey," Kalma said. She threw a wee piece of cornbread at her brother and it landed in his sculpted crewcut where it stayed for the remainder of the meal. Billy tried, for the next hour, to not stare at it.

"Dad gave me a book to read, Bookman. It's President Trump's memoir, *Grab Them by the Pussy: How to Get Ahead and, I'm Not Kidding Here, Stay Ahead.* You read it?"

Billy smiled a weak smile. Was he required to answer? The last book he read and liked was *The Great Gatsby* in college.

"This duck is ducky, Rasmus," Boils said, his sizeable mouth masticating the meat of an entire drumstick.

Billy was pretty sure Rasmus was not the poor cook's name. The cook was a middle-aged man with a face like a shiny nut. Where was Kissy? Had Kalma said 'Kissy?'

"Thank you, sir," the cook returned. He did not seem to take offense but rather to absorb the praise as his due.

"So, Willy—"

"Dadsy, stop it. You know his name is Billy."

The entire table was quiet but the smiles were painted on thinly.

"Of course, I do," Boils finally relented.

The conversation for the rest of the meal was mildly pleasant. Mrs. Voyles said little, smiling little moues into her plate, and every once in a while, raising her face toward Billy, whom she seemed not to recognize as part of her family. Billy ate little, such was the state of his nervous stomach. Kalma talked and giggled and looked altogether beautiful to her fiancé as she was bathed in the homey light of her family and her family's Xanadu-size kitchen fireplace.

After dinner, the family repaired to one of the estate's dens, where another fire, the magnitude of a small truck, roared in a mammoth oven. Billy was offered brandy which he took, having never tasted the stuff before.

"You like a good brandy?" Boils Voyles asked his wannabe son-in-law. Even this sounded minatory.

"Yessir," Billy said.

"Is this one?" Boils challenged.

Billy was nonplussed for a moment, searching his nearly empty store of experience for the proper response. "I believe so," he came out with.

Kalma sat on a hassock, her pretty legs splayed, her dress, naturally, hiked up to expose her panties, which tonight were as red as blood. Billy took pleasure in looking there, for comfort, for surcease from this painstaking evening, which threatened to last till the morn.

Tomboy came in once with a tray of small cakes, things Billy had never seen before, each one a clever little work of art, resembling Legos or Lincoln Logs. When he brought the tray to Kalma she took a long time deciding, the entire time holding Tomboy's free hand and working his fingers through hers affectionately. And, finally, when the gauntlet had been run, and the conversations were dwindling, everyone rose and Billy Kos was free to take his bride-to-be home.

"You will take good care of my Kalma," Mr. Voyles said. There was no uptalk. It was not a question.

"I will, sir," Billy said, reaching out his hand for the final shake, only to be left there awkwardly with it extended while Mr. Voyles kissed his daughter on the lips. He was a bit tipsy and the kiss was somewhere between paternal and vile. Then Kalma locked lips with Tomboy again, this time raising herself on tiptoe to put her arms around his neck. The family stood around and grinned.

"They've been like this since kids," Boils Voyles said, beaming with brandy and admiration.

"Heh heh," Arch said, archly. "Since kids."

Mrs. Voyles approached Billy and Billy feared he was next in line for a Voyles French kiss but she only meant to present her cheek for bussing. She stumbled slightly and their cheekbones barked.

"Ow," Renata Voyles said.

Finally, the engaged couple was in their car and on the way home.

"Don't you just love my family?" Kalma said, dreamily. "I am sure you do."

Billy did not answer and it didn't seem to matter.

"Isn't my mother beautiful? I think she is beautiful. And kind. It's where I get it, Billy Kos. It's in the blood. There are a lot of things that are in the blood."

"You and Tomboy sure seem close," Billy said.

"Tomboy, oh boy," Kalma said.

Kalma was absentmindedly running her fingers along the inside of one of her thighs.

"You always kiss like that?"

The interior of the darkened car took on some frost. Then Kalma slowly turned her head toward Billy.

"Is Billy Kos jealous?" she asked, her pretty lips curling upward.

"No," Billy said, too quickly. Should he admit the jealousy?

"Not of old Tomboy, oh boy," Kalma said. "He taught me how to French. Aren't you grateful? You can't be jealous."

"Of course not," Billy said.

When they got home Kalma had already undressed and fallen asleep by the time Billy came to bed. He lay next to her and stared at the ceiling for over an hour. The next day at the library, his first day there, he was almost too tired to absorb the many instructions he was given.

## CHAPTER EIGHTEEN

Within a week Billy had been fired. He could not get the coding right for the digital books. People expecting the latest Grisham or Frumkin would receive *Rear Wind: A History of Farting*, or *How to Build a Spaceship in your Backyard.*

"Billy Kos," his supervisor said, shaking his bald pate. "You're not really cut out for information distribution. Do you even read books?"

"I like biographies of TV stars," Billy said.

The face that his boss made could curdle milk.

"And poetry," he blurted.

"Whom do you read?"

Billy hesitated. It was a name. It was on the tip of his tongue. He'd heard talk of him. A Memphian. A famous poet.

"I like Camelove."

"Camelove," came back the parrot.

"Yes, Memphis writer."

"Camel Eros?"

Billy flushed. He'd been outed. He knew nothing. He was a C-minus student with no practical knowledge and a fiancé. Just shoot me, he thought.

"I'm afraid we'll have to go in a different direction," the supervisor said.

"I'm not sure what you mean," Billy Kos said.

"You're fired, Billy," his bald supervisor said, smiling.

Billy turned left when he walked out of the library. He was dazed and angry. He forgot his car and began to walk toward home. He was muttering but the mussitation in his head was even more elaborate. He kept picturing Kalma's face as he told her he no longer had a job. He was sure she wouldn't want to marry him.

"Billy Kos?" the female voice cracked the door to Billy's mind. It was coming from only a few feet away.

Billy looked up at a face that was familiar but not. A pretty face. Someone from college?

"It's Rita, Billy. Rita Someback. From high school."

Billy didn't need all those clues. He got it from 'Rita.'

"Rita," Billy said. He tried to invest his voice with some modicum of excitement.

"Well, I don't blame you if the name has negative associations."

Did it? Billy asked himself.

"I should never have hit you," Rita Someback said. "I'm glad you didn't have me arrested," she laughed. "Back then you couldn't hit people. Legally, I mean." She was now smiling and her eyes twinkled like gemstones.

"Rita," Billy said, more warmly. "Water under the bridge. Burnt. A burnt bridge."

Rita tittered. "Same old Billy. So funny."

Was he funny? Had he been funny back then? "Where are you on your way to?" Rita asked.

"No-nowhere," Billy said. He looked down the sidewalk for a clue.

"Let's get some coffee," Rita said, hooking her arm under his.

Once inside Java Joes, with their hot lattes in front of them, Billy began to feel a bit better. Then he remembered he was out of a job. And engaged.

"Sort of a redundant name, right?" Rita said.

Is my name redundant somehow?

"Like The Giant Behemoth, you know?"

Billy smiled into the mist around his head.

"Java Joes. Coffee coffees."

"Oh," Billy said.

"So, you seeing anyone?" Rita asked. She was wearing a small, gray mustache of foam.

"I see some people. From the old crowd, you mean?"

"Billy. Women. Do you have anyone special in your life now?"

"No, no no," Billy blurted. He had no idea why he denied Kalma so quickly, so effortlessly. He should want Rita to know that a woman loved him and wanted to marry him. What was he playing at?

"That surprises me, funny fellow like you."

"Funny. Yeah, that's not quite the turn-on some women pretend it is."

Rita thought about this as she sipped her coffee.

"That's very smart, Billy. But, really, at least in my case, funny is a big turn-on. Make me laugh and I'm yours," she said, saucily.

Billy looked harder at her twinkly eyes and nice cheekbones. She was pretty.

"These two popes walk into a bar," Billy said.

Rita's laugh was loud and paroxysmal. Billy couldn't help but laugh in return.

"I'm yours!" Rita shouted.

"Ha ha," Billy said. "Ha ha ha."

"Billy Kos, since you asked, I'm not seeing anyone either."

Now the silence was broken only by coffee sipping and the grinding of beans.

"So, are you working anywhere now, Billy?" Rita broke the silence. She probably realized she had promised more than she could deliver.

"Just got fired," Billy said, quickly.

"Ha ha ha! You kill me," Rita said.

Often the truth seems quite funny.

"It's true, I'm afraid," Billy added.

"Oh," Rita said. "I'm sorry. I thought you were making further jokes. To get into my pants." She laughed a tentative laugh.

"I wish," Billy said.

Rita looked Billy over. Her meditative glance was warm like a sunlamp.

"You wish you weren't fired or you wish you were getting into my pants?"

"Both," Billy said.

Rita laughed. "You are a bold Lochinvar," she said.

Billy didn't know what that was but it sounded like a woodnote coming out of Rita's sweet mouth.

"I can help you," Rita said.

Billy had to put his coffee down. His hand was shaking.

"First," Rita said, all business now. "I might have a job for you."

"Really?" Billy said. He was almost relieved that the conversation was not leading toward sexual pressure.

"Yes, and I can take you home with me, too. I live alone. Getting into my pants could not be easier."

Billy flushed, with both pleasure and fear.

"Listen, you remember my brother Hamm?"

Billy did not. "I think so," he said.

"He owns the new pot store down on Highland."

Marijuana had been legalized nationwide three years ago and the pot business was booming.

"High on your Horse, it's called," Rita said. "I told him the name would confuse people into thinking he offered heroin but he insisted it was clever. Most people just call it the pot store anyway."

"Ok," Billy said.

"You smoke much dope?" Rita asked.

"A little. In college."

"Hamm needs a full-time daytime clerk. He keeps the shop open at night and works the 3 to midnight shift himself. He needs someone who will work days."

"I can do that," Billy said.

"Do you know ditchweed from Thai stick?"

"What?" Billy asked.

"I thought so. Let's go to my place. I can teach you some things."

They went there in Rita's car. She lived in an apartment in a highrise near the Highland Strip, as it was once again called. You could see High on your Horse from her 8th floor window.

"This is nice," Billy said. It really was. Neat, clean, shiny.

"I can afford it," Rita said.

Once seated, with wine poured, Rita produced 7 boxes, each with different grades of marijuana. She proceeded to explain each and, with each explanation Billy was told to inhale one long hit. After they had tested all seven Billy began to sing "Jeremiah was a bullfrog," at the top of his voice.

"I sound pretty good," he said. "I also know all the words to 'Ride, Captain, Ride'. Oh, and 'I'm your Captain and Tennille.' Wait, is that the name of it?"

Rita fell off the couch laughing. She was lying on the floor laughing like a child. Her long legs were clad in skin tight jeans. They were so tight Billy could see that she was wearing no panties.

"Billy, now I'll show you how to get into my pants."

"Can we table that?" Billy said, suddenly sheepish and shy.

Rita made a fake pout. "Not quite the dish I was back in the day?"

"Oh, Rita, you're prettier than a red wagon. I'm engaged."

Rita hesitated. Then she sat up.

"Ah, Billy, sweet Billy. Sweet prevaricating Billy. Billy Liar, ha!" Rita straightened her spine and put on a sober expression. "Tell me all about her."

"Billy Kos, where have you been?" his fiancé asked when he got home.

"Had to work late," Billy said. "What's for dinner?" He began to snigger.

"Let's get Chink," Kalma said. "What do you smell like?"

"Books," Billy said. "It's old book smell. They should bottle it."

## CHAPTER NINETEEN

Billy did not immediately tell Kalma that he lost his job at the library and was peddling pot instead. He went off dutifully every morning with visions of hash balls in his head. The job was pretty easy and Billy was gradually learning the different varieties of weed. Hamm was an appreciative boss and Billy really had little to do each day. Often, between stoners, he read poetry. Since being fired from the library he wanted to become better read. He gravitated toward poetry because it was shorter. He had just about forgotten that he wrote some poor verses as a lad.

Then Arch visited the store.

"Well, well," Arch said. "How are you, Billy Boy?"

"Arch, listen," Billy began.

"Uh, Billy, you got any Erskine Caldwell? I need me something sexy."

"Arch, I," Billy began.

"Or no, maybe something spicier and spacier. Dr. Thompson, or *The Child's Garden of Grass.*" *The Child's Garden of Grass* was once a banned text but now was in wide circulation having been reprinted by the US Government Printing Office.

"Arch—for now, listen to me. Kalma doesn't know I got fired from the library."

"Fired, eh? That's rough, Billy Boy. Caught you feeling up the high school girls?"

"Huh, what? No, it was, just one of those things. You know—"

"I really don't, Billy Boy. You see, I've never had a job. My pop has more money than God or the late dearly-departed President Trump."

President Trump had been assassinated by an Italian immigrant named Matteo Matteo, using a shiny new Uzi he'd bought at Walmart, just after Trump had declared himself President for Life. At his arraignment Matteo said, "He was. He was president for life. I just shortened it for him." The two presidents since were ineffectual. They, like much of America, were scared of change, however innocuous a change might seem. Stasis ruled. People believed it was safe and comfortable.

"So, you can show me some compassion, right? It would be best. You know, for now."

"I'll think about it, Billy Boy. I'll run it through the old Voyles thought processor and see what turns up in my favor. Get me?"

Billy Kos stared at his future brother-in-law. He weighed both responses before he said, "Yes, I get you."

"Good. Gimme some Louisiana Local-Loco and one of those black balls of hash."

"Good choices," Billy said, sounding like a salesman for the first time.

"Thanks, Billy Boy. Charge it to my dad's account," Arch said, archly, turning on his fallen arches and showing Billy his back. Billy stood by, agape.

## CHAPTER TWENTY

> I barely knew I had skin before I met you.
> —Sarah Waters

The wedding went off with a hitch.

Kalma was wearing a white wedding dress so short it barely covered her pink panties ("something blue," she explained) and her perfect legs were bare and glowing. Billy wore a rented tux, light green with a fake rosebud boutonniere.

The witnesses were Kalma's parents. Her father had a grin, as false as dice, spread across his broad dark face. Her mother was a wax figurine.

The party after the wedding went on and on. A band, The Snit Pitchers, played old radio standards, "Joy to the World," "Heart of Glass," "More About Wendy Ward," "Florescent Sunset," "Peaceful Easy Feeling, "Cracklin' Rosie," "The Voice of Your Degeneration." They also covered the song that was ubiquitous in 2023, "The Wizard of Ozymandias," by Monkeys in Heaven. It was Kalma's favorite song: she told Billy it was 'their song.' Kalma danced like a devil on the head of a pin. She threw her arms toward the heavens. She shook her rounded bum. She purposely pulled her dress upward, her pink silk panties shining like the smile of an imp. Sometimes she even danced with her husband, who moved like a plow in a row of stones.

Willie came with a woman he met at the dog track. She had long black hair like Morticia and she looked at Kalma as if she had her all figured out and she smiled at Billy as if he needed her, Morticia, as if she held a key he had been seeking. Willie told Billy she held a degree in 'Fast Food Nutrition,' from Trump University.

There were friends of Kalma's there whom Billy had never before met. They were nice to him, sympathetic and friendly. Tomboy served drinks and some of the Voyles' other servants handled food. It was convivial. It was torture. Billy only wanted it to end so he could take his wife to the bed and breakfast in Covington, Tennessee, where they had booked a room for the night.

As midnight approached Billy Kos lost sight of his wife. He asked her friends, her mother, Willie. No one had seen her.

Finally, he found her in a small, dark hallway off the kitchen. She was standing on Tomboy's shoes, as if she were his daughter learning to dance, and Tomboy's large, strong hands were holding her hips as if to guide her home. Billy didn't know if he'd come too late or too early.

"Hello, husband," Kalma said. "I was just saying goodbye to Tomboy. I hope you're ready to leave."

"I am," Billy said. "Goodbye, Tomboy."

"Goodbye, Mr. Kos," Tomboy said. He kissed Kalma quickly on the cheek.

"This is only the beginning," Boils Voyles said, at the car, pressing a thousand-dollar bill into Billy's hand. Billy didn't know if the money was the beginning or if his father in law was referring to their new marital pact.

The drive to Covington took a long hour. Kalma lay back in her seat, singing softly to herself, one hand resting on her husband's thigh.

Billy had an erection the entire ride and it rendered him almost speechless.

"Here we go," he said, nonsensically, about halfway through the drive.

"We're married," Kalma said. "Hmm, hmm. Mrs. Billy Kos."

"My wife," Billy said.

Their room at the bed and breakfast was over a horse stable. There were no other rooms. It was a one-room bed and breakfast. There didn't seem to be anyone around for miles. They let themselves in with a key they had purchased weeks ago. The room they entered was as large as a barn, high raftered ceilings of old wood, a bear rug on a spacious wooden floor, a television the size of a 7/11, a shiny kitchen off one side, and a bedroom off the other. The bedroom was nearly as big as the living room and the bed a giant's. The bathroom off the bedroom was all bright yellow tile and old iron fixtures.

"Wheee," Kalma said, as they walked into the bedroom. "Billy Kos!"

"Are you pleased, my wife?" Billy asked, putting his arms around her and kissing her deeply.

"It's dreamy, isn't it, Billy Kos?"

"It is, my dear. Happy honeymoon."

"It is a honeymoon, isn't it, my love?"

"It is, Kalma. Tonight, it begins."

"Hm, do you think married sex is different from single sex?" Kalma said, with a comic frown. She moved a hand toward her mouth but Billy interrupted it and pulled Kalma's lower lip himself.

"I have no idea," Billy said.

"I know you're ready, Billy. I felt you."

"Yes, my love."

"Oh, Billy! I have a surprise! Strip out of that beautiful suit and I'll meet you on the bed!"

She disappeared into the bathroom with her little bag. She closed the door.

Billy undressed down to his underwear. He lowered the lights in the room. He was tired and a bit worried about how well he would perform but he was also as horny as a civet.

"Here I come!" Kalma called from inside the bathroom.

Kalma came out wearing a tight blue slip and nothing else. The way it hugged her curvy hips made Billy Kos hurt. He loved her with a passion he had never dreamed himself capable of. She stood in the doorway and cocked a hip to one side the way she thought models did.

"My wife," Billy said.

"Do I look real sexy, Billy Kos? Do I?"

"You have no idea, Kalma."

"I am, aren't I? I'm real sexy."

Billy laughed at his wife.

"Come to me, wife," he said.

"Billy, I have no panties on."

"I know, dear."

"I'm like some high-priced whore, aren't I?"

"Do you want to be, darling?"

"For tonight, yes, Billy Kos. For our first married night."

"Then you are. You're more beautiful than a morning star."

"Let's do it now, Billy. I'm really wet."

When Kalma pushed Billy backward and leapt onto him she pressed her bare wet crotch against the front of Billy's briefs, grinding down on his erection.

"Whooee," she said. "You feel like a husband."

"Let's not go too fast, Love. I'm about to burst already."

"Really, Billy Kos? You want me that bad, don't you?"

She dismounted, turned 180 degrees, and sat back on top of his erection. Her slip rode up over her hips and, as she moved her hips over him, Billy was entranced by the beauty of her bare backside. She put her hand underneath herself and pulled Billy's cock out of his briefs and pushed herself down on it hard.

"Ahhh," she said. "Billy. My Billy Kos."

"Kalma, I, Kalma—mm," Billy began and then suddenly he was coming inside her, a powerful and long-lasting orgasm, like a hose after the kinks been shaken out of it.

"Ackackacak," Billy said, his body spuming.

"Billy!" Kalma said. "You came already!"

After he caught his breath Billy said, "I'm sorry, Kalma. It was building all night."

"It's ok," Kalma said. "We can do it some more."

Billy closed his eyes hard and when he opened them there were stars on the ceiling.

"I-I'm not sure about twice in one night," Billy said. It was a confession in preparation for a marriage rife with them, Billy thought. All my insecurities will be uploaded.

"Billy Kos, this is our wedding night. Of course you can make another boner."

Her confidence in him shook him. She was ridiculous.

"Come here, babe," she said, dismounting. Downstairs a horse neighed.

"Don't say nay to me, Mr. Ed," Kalma said. She pulled the slip off over her head and then, like a nurse tidying up, removed Billy's retted briefs.

"Let's just see what's what," she said.

"Oh Kalma," Billy said. "I do love you so."

"I know, Billy Kos. Now, go down on me."

Billy did. His wife's crotch was an admixture of her personal funk, which he'd come to know intimately, and his bleachy spunk.

When he found her clit with his tongue and bore down Kalma had a nice, rocking orgasm.

"Husband, husband, husband," she cooed as she came.

Billy kept his mouth loosely pressed to her dripping pubic hair. His tongue flicked lazily around her.

"Wow, that's a good first married orgasm," Kalma said. "Now come up here."

Billy did as instructed. Kalma put a hand on each side of his head and held his face tightly.

"Now listen closely, husband. I am going to have another orgasm or two and I want them to be from fucking. Ok? So, we're gonna get your little wiggler hard again."

Billy wanted to weep. But as his wife began to lick him and tickle his balls and finger his anus Billy's cock began to swell again. It hurt a bit but it was every bit as hard as the first time

"Now," Kalma said.

And all went well. They did it in 6 ½ different ways and Kalma came four more times and Billy twice. As they lay in each other's arms the sun was rising and Billy's cock hurt and Kalma fell asleep on Billy's chest, a thin line of drool escaping her mouth.

Billy was feeling righteous and pure. He was feeling like a married man and like a stud. Maybe all married men felt this way, he thought.

And just then, in her sleep, Kalma said, 'Thank you, Tomboy."

## CHAPTER TWENTY-ONE

The couple honeymooned on the tiny island of Great Abaco, the excursion a gift from Boils, of course. Great Abaco was, naturally, larger than Little Abaco. Boils told them no one vacationed there anymore, ever since the U.S. went to war against them in 2021, kicked out the Free Independent party members, and told Britain that Abaco was now an American protectorate.

They flew to Key West and from there were taken by a twin-engine plane with *Voyles* written on the side in gilt Harlow Solid

Italic. When Billy and Kalma arrived on the tiny island the place seemed deserted, a ghostly landmass. A bedraggled gypsy picked them up in a beat-up 1972 Duster.

"Mr. Voyles?" the gaunt fellow inquired.

"Kos. Billy, and my wife Kalma."

"Of course," the driver said, opening the back door for them.

He drove at about 15 miles an hour through a tiny hamlet that once must have looked lovely, with gingerbread houses and small markets and eateries. Many were boarded up now and the road's pavement was cracked and jagged. They bounced along on the narrow road like a cartoon jalopy on overstressed springs. The makeshift hack pulled up in front of a two-story building in what remained of the town square. In bright smaragdine letters a sign above the door declared the place Holiday Inn.

"Not quite what Kemmons had in mind," Billy remarked.

His wife wrinkled her freckled nose, squinted under the high bright sun and her floppy white sunhat, and shrugged her shoulders. "I bet the rooms are nice," she said.

The room they were shown to was indeed nice. The lobby, which looked like a cheap set from a 1950s TV series, held one occupant, apparently a desk clerk, because he was behind a desk. He looked up from the paper he was reading and smiled as the cabbie showed the couple up the stairs, stopping in front of room 202.

"Here ya go," he said, in an unreadable accent.

"Why not 201?" Billy asked, with a grin. His attempts at affability often fell short.

"201 bad room," the fellow said.

Billy put a bill of large denomination in the fellow's hand.

"For taxi service and bellboying," Billy said, smiling.

The gaunt man looked at the bill and a smile grew on his unhandsome face. "You call Elbow you need anything else," he said, backing quickly away.

Billy smiled wider. The fellow was really quite clownish.

"Did he say Elbow?" Billy asked no one, because his wife had swept into the room and was dancing around amid its spacious, if tacky, ornamentation. It looked like a cross between a Las Vegas Egyptian knockoff and a Memphis whorehouse.

"It's tweedly pretty!" Kalma said, as she pirouetted. Billy put the bags down, closed the door, and watched his new spouse dance like a sozzled reveler.

"I'm pleased you're pleased," Billy said. "Mrs. Kos."

"Mrs. Kos," Mrs. Kos parroted. "I am Mrs. Kos!"

"What do you want to do first, Darling?" Billy asked, still standing next to the luggage. "Are you tired from the trip or do you want to walk around the village?"

"Or look for something to eat?" she asked, mid-piqué turn.

"Are you hungry, Darling?" Billy asked, still standing next to the luggage, still smiling at his wife's giddy prancing.

"I'm always hungry Husband. Are you a hungry husband?"

"I could eat. Did you see anything on the ride in, any place to eat?"

Now Kalma slowed her turns, winding down, until she eventually stopped. She put a finger to her lip.

"I didn't," she said. "That's kinda weird, isn't it?"

"I get the feeling this little burg has seen better days."

"Yes, yes, they must have."

"We could do scouting."

"Scouting," Kalma repeated.

"Sure, a nice walk would be good."

Kalma was thinking. "Have you seen the bed?" she asked.

Billy now walked around the room a bit, a faux-show of intelligence gathering. He stopped at the bedroom's door. Inside was a bed the size of a small battleship, with a gold lame bedspread and tall, carved bedposts supporting a canopy which was painted to resemble the heavenly vaults.

"My," he said.

"Nice big bed, Husband," Kalma said.

"I thought you were hungry," Billy said, turning and putting his arms around his wife.

"I could eat," she said. "Later."

## CHAPTER TWENTY-TWO

In walking around the village, they made a quick diagnosis. The buildings remaining, which still housed going concerns, were outnumbered by the failed businesses by about 20 to 1. All the buildings, abandoned or still lit, wore a plank board suit like a hobo's defiled garments. Much of the wood needed paint and, in some places, had rotted in the salty air. They found two restaurants. One boasted "Best Island Fair," and was called "Mac's." The other, a tad farther away and closer to the island's lone public beach, was called "American Home Cooking." They chose Mac's for their evening meal.

But first they went shopping, if shopping it could be called. More like foraging in the detritus of a failed township. There were seashells galore, some with pasted-on googly eyes, some painted unnatural colors. This perhaps was all that was left of the island's artistic culture.

"This is nice," Kalma said. She was holding a conch shell in her hands. In the shell's declivity was glued a stuffed troll who was giving the finger. The troll wore a shirt that said, "Yankees Come Home."

"I don't understand it," Billy said.

Kalma shrugged and set it back down.

"How about this?" she now asked, brandishing a piece of driftwood which had 8 of the 10 commandments painted on it.

"I guess they don't care about false witness or coveting," Billy said with a grin.

"There are only eight real commandments," Kalma said. She stuck her bottom lip out, which was either pugnaciousness or pouting.

"I'm pretty sure there are ten."

Kalma looked at it seriously. "Oh," she said. "Maybe they aren't Christians."

"Maybe they ran out of room."

"Yes," Kalma said, thinking about it. "That's what happened, Billy Kos."

They wandered into another shop that sold snorkeling gear, surfboards and diving equipment. It was the most modern place they encountered and the blond Aryan behind the counter, his broad, muscular, hairy chest exposed inside an open fringe vest, greeted them cheerily with a British accent, and a shaka sign.

"How are you folks?" he asked.

"Fine, fine," Billy said. He looked quickly around the shop and surmised that there was nothing there for him.

"Oh, Billy, can we snorkel?" Kalma asked, resting her hand on a display of snorkels and masks.

"I don't know, Love. It might be dangerous. I have no idea how to do that," Billy said, his voice rising into a feminine squeak. He was embarrassed to be expressing his qualms in front of the Adonis, who was obviously a man of the sea, a modern Nemo, a small-town Kelly Slater. He just stood there smiling with all his teeth, which gleamed like dragon scales.

"We can learn," Kalma said, coquettishly cocking her hip and shifting from one foot to the other. "I bet he can show us." She smiled at the Viking.

"Of course," he said. He just stood there smiling with all his teeth.

Billy Kos leered an apprehensive grin at the man and then a cockeyed one at his wife.

"It's almost dinner time," Billy said.

"Tomorrow's good," the god spoke.

"Tomorrow. . ." Billy said as if he had a meeting.

"I wake up early. How's 7 right out there?" He pointed through his open door at the landmass's solitary clean beach.

"Ooh, yes," Kalma said. "Thank you!"

"Jason," the god said, proffering a beautiful, meaty hand.

"Of course," Billy said. "Billy Kos. And this is my wife Kalma."

The hand swallowing Billy's was wringing it of all fluids. He let go and Billy's hand dropped to his side as if lifeless. Now Jason took

Kalma's hand much more gently in his, and smiled with all his teeth while looking Kalma in the eye.

"Kalma," he said. "I'll see you two in the morning."

The menu at Mac's was a mishmash of seafood and Ethiopian cuisine.

"Why Ethiopian?" Billy said, scanning the menu.

"Maybe the owner is from Ethiopia," Kalma said. She was glowing. Billy looked at her bright eyes, and chunky, freckly cheeks and fell in love with her all over again.

"You mean Mac?" he said. His smile was an oyster shell.

"Haha, Billy Kos," Kalma said, hitting him with her menu.

Billy ordered Conch Wat over Injera, and Kalma went for the Oysters Berbere and a side of Oysters in Niter Kibbeh. The food arrived 45 minutes later but it was steaming hot and quite delicious. Their waiter, a small, plump man who spoke broken English nodded at everything they said, possibly comprehending nothing.

"This was excellent," Billy Kos said, as the waiter began to clear the table. "Send Mac my compliments."

"Mac?" the waiter said.

"The owner?"

"Mac?" he repeated as if he'd never heard the word before. "Ah, the chef!" he said it as if there was a 'v' at the end.

Moments later a dark, handsome gentleman was at their side.

"Everything happy?" he asked.

"Are you Mac?"

"Ha ha, you Americans like your little jokes. There is no Mac of course. It is short for MacDonald's, an American institution I believe. Did the food not please you?"

He stood slightly inclined at the waist.

"It was wonderful," Billy hastened to say.

"Fantastic," Kalma added.

"Why do you wish to complain then?"

"We don't. We didn't. We asked the waiter if he would send our compliments to the chef."

"Ah I see. He does not understand your heavy accents."

"The food was wonderful. You are an artist," Kalma said.

"You are very kind, Madam. I will send you a complimentary dessert."

"Thank you!" Kalma said, smiling at Billy as if she were twelve years old.

The dessert had an Ethiopian name that neither caught. It looked like eyeballs in a gelatinous dairy product. And it tasted like aquarium water.

## CHAPTER TWENTY-THREE

Meeting Jason on the beach at 7 a.m. was just about the last thing Billy wanted to do. They made love upon returning to the honeymoon bower after dinner and it was slow and sexy and just the loveliest thing Billy could imagine. They fell asleep with one of Kalma's superlative legs across Billy's midsection.

And now, upon awaking, Billy did not want to leave the bed for any reason. He gently stroked his wife's cross-thigh while gathering wool. Her skin was soft as the light leaking around the thin shade. It was the luciferous ocean. Billy imagined he could smell the brackish dash in the air. He was happy.

They made it to the beach without first breakfasting. There was a small buffet off the lobby but it had been well picked over and they were running behindhand.

Jason was already on the beach when they arrived. He looked like a deity transplanted to the terraqueous domain. His chest hair was a country unto itself; the sweat was already gathering around his golden hairs like tiny rills. His smile looked like an expensive piano.

"Good morning, Koses," he boomed.

In each hand he held a mask and snorkel set.

"I charged these to your room. I 'ope that's ok," he boomed.

"Fine," Billy said. "You know where we're staying?"

Jason looked at Billy with a just-between-us smile.

"Oh, right. Where else?"

"Show me how to put that on," Kalma said, stepping forward.

"That's my girl," Jason said.

After fitting the apparatuses on each of the Koses he told them briefly how to float on the surface and let the action happen below. Once each of them floated in around two feet of water just off shore Jason bade them stand.

"Now, 'ow to dive deeper to get to the real show, the reefs and the ocean floor. It's simple but you have to concentrate. Don't breathe in. Okay, mates?"

Now they waded further out till the water was up to their oxters and Jason's lower chest. They floated.

Billy's mask felt like it was cutting the sides of his face. He was sure he was going to be marked for life. Clearly the suction was dangerous. Then, slowly, the sea began to calm him. He was holding Kalma's hand and when he looked at her she was watching the ocean floor as if it were Munchkinland suddenly appearing in living color. He squeezed her hand but she was rapt. Billy refocused on the show.

There were small creatures all around him, fish mostly. Small yellow fish were abundant. He vowed when he got back to Memphis to study fish, to be able to name all that he saw. There was a flounder on the bottom, moving like a Roomba. At first Billy thought it was a stingray and, in his excitement and desire to cue in his wife he took a deep breath. The amount of seawater that flowed into his lungs was extraordinary. Billy blew out instinctually and managed to clear his pipe but he had to surface for air anyway. He let go of Kalma's hand.

When he resubmerged Kalma was on her way up. In a split second, she shot back past him, swimming further out. He watched her kick and descend, her body a thing of immaculate splendor. She seemed a creature of the deep herself, a silkie, or mermaid. Kalma was headed for deeper water so Billy followed.

Together they began to descend on a reef which was teeming with life. From above it looked like Atlantis, a conurbation of iridescence and shimmering light and wonder, a chromaticity. Off to their left they saw Jason already examining the reef. Billy took Kalma's hand again and she turned to him. Her eyes were wide. Her smile was wider. She was ecstatic.

They stayed down as long as they could and then swam upward together.

"Wowie zowie, Billy Kos!" Kalma said, kicking her legs to stay buoyant. She pulled her mask off her face. "This is magic!"

"It's quite beautiful," Billy said. "And so are you."

"Oh, Billy Kos, how I love you."

"I love you, too, Kalma. You are my everything."

"Hey, you two," Jason said, joining their floating conference.

"Did you see it?"

"It's gorgeous," Billy said.

"But deadly."

"You mean because it can cut you?"

"Wait, we're talking about two different things. Yes, the coral can cut you. I forgot to say that. I'm a bad coach. No, I meant the eel."

"Eek, eel!" Kalma said.

"Yes, eek," Jason replied. "They can bite like a bloody shark."

"Really?" Billy said. He was hoping the Argonaut was pulling their legs.

"Really," Jason said. "It'll move away."

"So should we," Billy said. Suddenly it seemed like a point of honor to him, to protect his wife. "Let's swim in, Kalma."

Kalma made a faux pout and reluctantly began to swim to shore. Once all three were on the beach Kalma began to spread the towels out for them to lie on. She and Billy both had dressed in swimming suits and t-shirts. Now she stripped off her shirt and her brief bikini-clad body, in all its curvaceous wonder, was revealed.

Well," Jason said.

Billy looked at him, his maleness still soaring, but Jason did not meet his eye. He was openly ogling Kalma.

"You're quite beautiful," he said.

"Thank you," Kalma said. "The water made my nipples stand out."

Billy died a little inside.

Jason laughed. "Sure enough," he said.

## CHAPTER TWENTY-FOUR

That afternoon Billy was not feeling up to snuff; he was bilious, irritable. Though they had been smart enough to wear t-shirts while snorkeling they had still absorbed more of the sun than they were used to. Ever since America had broken with the other countries over the carbon emissions agreement Americans had learned to fear the sun. There were worse things than sun sickness but, still, Billy sat on the toilet grieving for his lost health. The bathroom smelled like brine and some kind of orangey soap.

"I've never had this before," he said through the open door. "I guess I got overheated."

"Are you having a BM?" Kalma inquired from the bed where she lay on top of the covers reading a Vogue magazine that was seven months old.

"Something like that," Billy said. "Want me to close the door?"

"Hmm, hmm," Kalma hummed.

"Kalma?"

"Yes, dear. No, leave it open. We can talk this way."

"Thank you. Oh, oh."

"My poor Billy Kos."

"I don't know if I'll feel like going out to eat."

"Oh. What should we do for food then?"

"I think they have room service."

"But there is no restaurant in the hotel."

"Yes, but I swear—oh, oh—that I saw something about room service. Is there something on the dresser there?"

"Wait. Oh, yes, there is a room service menu."

"Ok, let's call them in a bit and we can stay in and watch TV on the bed."

"Ok, husband."

Later Billy felt a tad better. The eddying air from the ceiling fan over the bed felt wonderful.

"What do you want?" Kalma asked, scanning the brief menu. "They actually have a hamburger and fries."

"Yes, that's what I want. No seafood tonight."

"I want seafood. Lots of fried seafood. I'll call."

"Hello?" the voice on the other end of the telephone said.

"Hi. This is Kalma in room 202."

"Yes, ma'am," the voice said. What kind of accent was that? It sounded like ersatz European.

"We'd like room service."

There was silence.

"You know, food. Dinner."

Silence.

"Can we get food delivered to our room?"

"Oh, yes ma'am. Food service. We do that. We get it from nearby restaurant."

"Ok," Kalma said. "One hamburger and fries and one fried seafood platter."

"What?"

Kalma repeated the order. "Oh, I better write this down. Hold please."

Once the order was placed Kalma turned on the television. There were two channels. One was the weather channel and one boasted "Sports and Movies! 24/7!" They were showing a lacrosse match.

"Oh ugh," Kalma said.

"Should we fool around instead?"

"Billy Kos is feeling better. Yes?

"Yes, much better, Darling. Come here."

He kissed her lips, cheek, neck. His hand found a nipple.

"Billy Kos, we don't have time for this."

"You're right. But I'm all stirred up."

"After dinner."

"I might be too full."

"Billy, you know that's a poor thing to say to your wife on your honeymoon."

"You're right, Darling. I apologize. After dinner."

After an hour of lacrosse and old magazines Billy picked up the phone again.

"Hello?"

"Room 202. We ordered some food."

"Yessir."

"It's not here yet."

"I understand," the voice said with bland calm.

"Is it coming soon?"

"What did you order?"

"Hamburger. Seafood platter."

"I better write this down."

Billy slammed the phone down. "I don't think food is coming."

"Oh, Billy Kos! I'm hungry."

"I'll shower and get dressed. We'll have to go out."

"I'm all ready. Shall I go fetch?"

"No, really, I'll be ready in a flash."

"I'll go, Billy Kos. I'll bring back food."

Kalma bounced off the bed and was gone.

Billy tried to follow lacrosse.

An hour later the station switched to Movies. Tonight's first offering was *Pretty in Pink*. A classic, the pre-movie teaser said.

About an hour into *Pretty in Pink* Billy decided he better go look for his wife. He began to dress and the phone rang.

"Billy Kos," Kalma said. "I will be late bringing food."

"What? Where are you?"

"At the restaurant, Silly."

"How late? What's the problem?"

"Really late, ok? Hold your horses, Billy Kos."

At 11:15 Kalma returned, brandishing a brown grocery bag, apparently full of food.

"I bet you're gonna love this food," she said.

"Where have you been?"

"I called," Kalma said.

"I know. That was hours ago."

Kalma stuck out her protuberant lower lip. "Don't ruin our dinner, Husband."

Billy was angry. He was also hungry and tired.

"Yes, yes," he said.

"Here's your hamburger and they didn't have fries so they added squid, I think. Something in ink." Kalma giggled. "That rhymed."

"Where's your dinner?

"Oh, I decided I wasn't hungry."

By the time Billy had eaten his hamburger, and the television was halfway through *Slam Dunk Ernest,* Kalma was curled up on the covers, asleep, with her thumb in her mouth.

## CHAPTER TWENTY-FIVE

The next morning, they strolled into another part of town that had a few more shops, a grocery, a barber and a small bookstore. Some of the shutters and doors were painted pastel colors, pale pink, indigo blue. This neighborhood, though only perpendicular to the main street and two blocks away, seemed in another country. It was almost as if the natives, or what was left of them, had all huddled here away from the hotel and restaurants.

Billy and Kalma made plans to return to the bookstore after they ate breakfast. And, for breakfast, they bought some bread, cheese and plantains from the grocery store. The woman there, who only had one eye—the other socket was bare and sunken—smiled a jagged smile and nodded after everything they said.

"Eh, eh," she said, pleasantly.

On their bed the honeymooners spread out the food and ate with their fingers.

"Plantains are good," Kalma said. She playfully put the tip on the edge of her lips and slid it slowly in.

"Oh, wife," Billy said, half-laughing and half-choking.

"Billy Kos," Kalma said.

"After the bookstore what do you want to do?"

"Hm, hm, how about snorkeling?"

"Well—" Billy began.

"Jason's off the island for the day."

Billy Kos stopped chewing.

"How do you know that?"

"He told me."

"When, Kalma, did Jason tell you that?"

"Last night. I met him when I was walking to the restaurant. Did you know he owns his own plane? And he's like a surf champion or something. And that he graduated from Skidmore with a degree in Jewish Literature."

"You had quite a talk."

"He walked with me a bit."

"A long bit?"

"A bit is short, isn't it? A long bit would be an oxymoron."

"Did y'all go to the restaurant together?"

"Jewish Literature. Doesn't that seem an odd area of concentration?"

"Kalma, did you and Jason eat together last night."

Kalma studied her husband's face for a bit. A short bit.

"What are you meaning, Husband? Do you think I had sexual relations with Jason?"

"Kalma, no," Billy Kos said quickly. Though that is exactly what he meant.

"I told you I wasn't hungry last night."

"Ok." Now Billy wasn't hungry. He pushed the bread and cheese away.

"Would you be upset if I had sexual relations with Jason, Husband?"

"What? Of course I would."

"Hm, that's good to know, I guess."

"What do you think, Kalma? Wouldn't you be upset if I had sexual relation—sex, with someone else?"

"Like Jason? Have you ever fantasized about being with a man?"

"No," Billy said, though he had, but it was long ago.

"Then I wouldn't be jealous," Kalma concluded. She began to gather the refuse of their bed picnic.

"Wait, Kalma. Did you have sex with Jason last night?"

"It's our honeymoon, Billy Kos," Kalma said, disappearing quickly into the bathroom and closing the door.

Billy stewed. He sat and stewed.

Kalma emerged wearing the bikini in which she looked downright succulent. Billy wanted her suddenly so badly that his erection was unexpected and painful. He also felt a little ill. Had another man touched those nipples? Had that Viking, who admired them, suckled at them the night before?

"Penny for your thoughts, Billy Kos."

Billy smiled a smile as weak as a wrinkle.

"I was thinking about shopping for books," Billy said.

"Good then, let's wear our suits under our clothes and carry our snorkels with us in the beach bag."

"Of course," Billy said.

The bookstore was small, cramped and dusty. A lot of used paperbacks, most likely left behind by tourists. Some were swollen like over-ripe roses. The store, called City Writes Bookstore, did have a nice wall of first editions, mostly American authors of the mid-twentieth century. Billy scanned that wall pretty thoroughly and found a nice copy of Zora Neal Hurston's *Tell My Horse*, a rare first but in pretty poor shape, its hinge hanging precipitously. And the price was more than Billy was prepared to pay for it.

"Looky here, Billy Kos," Kalma said. She was holding up a beat-up copy of Franz Kafka's *Amerika*. "Isn't this someone you studied?"

"Hm, Kafka, no, I don't think so."

"You did. You told me."

"Franz Boas. Anthropology. Coincidentally I was just looking at a Zora Neal Hurston first edition. She studied with Boas. And that's about all I remember."

Kalma had already moved away. She was pulling at her lower lip. Had he hurt her feelings by correcting her? She was now scanning a copy of *The Story of O.*

"What's that, Darling?" Billy asked, moving closer to her.

"Nothing. I don't know," Kalma sulked.

They left the bookstore with only two paperbacks. Billy bought a Leon Uris novel, water-distended to almost twice its already monumental bulk. And Kalma took *The Story of O.*

"Snorkeling now?" Billy asked, reaching for his wife's hand. She gave it to him half-heartedly and he ended up holding only the tips of her fingers.

"You mad at me?"

Kalma let her hand slip out of his. She hummed a couple times.

"Kalma?"

"I don't see Jason," she said, as they crossed the hot asphalt road and the beach came into view.

"Disappointed?"

"Mm, I dunno. He has a nice stomach."

Billy's ire was immediate. He flushed red. He saw red.

"That's nice," he spat.

"It is. He has this little line of hair that leads from his belly button down to his pubes."

Billy stopped on the edge of the sand. He threw the beach bag down.

"How far down does it go, Kalma?" Billy's voice shook.

"All the way, Billy Kos, of course."

"Kalma, what are you telling me?"

"That pubic hair is sexy, I guess."

"For fuck's sake," Billy sputtered. He faltered for a moment and then he ran from her. He hit the surf hard, kicking off his khaki shorts but without stripping off his t-shirt.

Kalma watched him for a moment and then she sat next to the beach bag. She pulled out *The Story of O.* She read.

After about ten minutes Billy came back, wadding his wet t-shirt into an angry ball and angrily kicking his shorts which lay in the sand in front of him, like a disgorged sea creature. This dislodged his wallet from their pocket and Billy had to stoop to pick it up, essentially spoiling what was a grand show of spite.

He threw himself down next to his wife. She read on.

"Ok," Billy said. "Tell me everything."

Kalma put her finger in the book and looked at her husband. Her jaw was set; a cruel line ran from her chin to cheek.

"What would you like to hear, Husband?"

"What happened with you and the Argonaut. You didn't eat dinner with him, did you?" It was not what he meant to ask, giving her the opportunity to answer a less incriminating question.

"No dinner. We went back to his place."

Billy felt sick. He didn't want to hear this.

"Why? Why would you do that?"

"Billy Kos, because he invited me." The cruel line was crueler. It was a terrible line.

"Just go ahead," Billy said, lying back on the hot sand and closing his eyes.

"He was only wearing a bathing suit." Kalma paused to guage the effect of this. Billy did not move. "So, I told him I liked his belly button hair. Because I couldn't take my eyes off it. It was golden and his skin was soft brown. It like, *glowed.*

"Jason said, 'Feel it, it's soft'."

"Where were you?" Billy Kos mumbled.

"Standing in his kitchen."

"I won't interrupt again."

"So, I put a finger to it and ran it up and down. He kind of sighed. And then he said it." Kalma paused. She threw the book into the beach bag. "He said, 'It goes all the way down to my pubes.' So, I said, of course, 'that's nice,' and he said, 'look,' and he untied the little tie-ey thing to his suit and lowered it. I said, 'mm hm,' and he said, 'all the way,' and I put my finger to it and ran it down to the thicker bush of his pubic hair and so he let his suit drop."

Billy groaned.

"I'll stop now, Billy Kos. I'm sorry. I was mad for a minute but I'm not mad now."

"Tell me everything," Billy growled through grit teeth.

Kalma sighed, petulantly. "His dick was semi-hard, you know, like you in the morning when we wake up, and I said, 'you have a pretty dick,' and he said, 'Kalma, I'm going to undress you now.' And he pulled my dress off over my head. I wasn't wearing a bra and he said, 'you really have astonishing nipples, I couldn't stop thinking about them after you pointed them out on the beach,' and I said, 'thank you, Jason,' and he kicked off his trunks and picked me up in his arms and kissed me long and hard. He kinda kisses like Tomboy, with a lot of tongue, you know? Hm hm, anyway, he reached for my panties and I stopped him. I said, 'I'm on my honeymoon, Bucko.' And that made him pull back. He stood there in his nakedness and his dick was pretty hard by now."

Kalma stopped. "Well—" she said, apropos of nothing.

"You fucked him. On our honeymoon." Billy asked his tears not to come but they came anyway. He did not sob but tears ran down each cheek, little embarrassing, silent trickles.

"I did NOT," Kalma said. "I told you I told him I was on my honeymoon."

"But, but, you still saw him naked and kissed him."

"Yes, I did that. And I sucked him off."

"Kalma!" Billy shouted. Far down the beach an old woman and what must have been her grandchildren looked up from their sandcastle.

"Billy Kos, it was just a blowjob. It was like a vacation thing, you know? Like you do on spring break?"

"I never went to spring break."

"Well, there you go," Kalma said, as if that settled it.

"You sucked off a stranger on our honeymoon."

"Yes, Billy, I did. It wasn't like we had sex. Then he fingered me till I came. Then I told him I had to get your dinner. Ok. See, I had to get your dinner."

Billy rose slowly. Only then did he realize how much the hot sand had burned his back. He walked slowly back to the hotel. Kalma did not follow him. He didn't know whether he wanted her to or not.

## CHAPTER TWENTY-SIX

> The poem is nothing but information. It is the Constitution of the inner country.
>
> —Leonard Cohen

The flight back to Memphis was uneventful. Billy changed seats with a Marine a few rows up and let him sit next to his cheating wife. He could have her. "Tell it to the Marines," Billy cogitated.

When they landed Billy went to the luggage carousel by himself. By the time he'd gotten both bags Kalma had found a cab and gone home. Billy found another cab.

"Take me anywhere but home," he told the cabbie.

Later that night, when he returned, it was the beginning of the cold, brutal part of his marriage.

Billy began sleeping in his old bedroom. There was still a small piece of fishing line hanging from a nail in the ceiling from which he had appended a plastic model airplane he built. There were still tape marks on the walls from where he'd mounted rock star posters: NOTS, The Stranglers, Al Green, The Snit Pitchers, Jism, Hendrix. His bed was his narrow twin and there was a Mexican serape at the foot, a gift from a cousin who had vacationed in Mexico.

Billy also began two activities relatively new to the adult he had reluctantly become: reading and writing poetry. He went to Burke's Book Store, the 185+ year-old Memphis landmark, and cherry-picked their poetry section. He came home with W. S. Merwin, Anne Sexton, James Royce, John Berryman, Bobby Rogers, Mary Oliver and *The Selected Poems of Camel Jeremy Eros*. In bed at night, he propped a yellow legal pad on his knees and began writing random lines. He had no idea how to create a poem from start to finish, to create a shapely verse that worked like a small clock. He filled the sheets with sentences, some swiped from the poets he was voraciously reading, some random words that flashed across his mind-screen.

Some nights he brought home new varieties of weed from the store and tried writing when stoned. These were poor abortions, children begun in love and what seemed to be bright insight, but which withered and died before naissance.

The first poem he thought might be a finished poem was entitled, "Kalma on the Killing Floor." It wasn't pretty. But it had *something*, an energy, negative but crackling, sending off sparks like a struck anvil.

After six weeks, the married couple began to eat meals together again. The talk was phatic and the raw emotions still an unhealthy undercurrent but they sat together and, at least, acknowledged each other as human beings.

One night Kalma tried to open a small hole in the ice. She said, "Billy Kos, I don't understand why you're so upset with me."

Billy hesitated, then lifted his plate of lentils and rice and went to his room to eat and stew. He began a poem he called "I don't understand why you're so upset with me." It went well for a while and then petered out. He vowed to return to it the next day.

Soon, Billy had collected about 25 (or 27) 'finished' poems. Poems he had gone over and over until the words were little tangled fishing lines. He didn't think 25 made a book and he didn't know what to do with them. He called Willie, with whom he'd lost contact slightly, marriage making for him and for Willie a refuge from the outer world and a place where friends, for a little while, were not as necessary. Willie had married a woman he met at The Church of Scientology, which Willie had joined only to meet women. Her name was Aphrodite Springsteen and she had large breasts (a must, according to Willie), bucked teeth, magenta hair and a tattoo on one bicep which read "Scientology is the study of knowingness."

They were married by Tom Cruise, the same minister who presided over Costa Kos's funeral.

"Hey, Buddy," Willie answered his phone.

"Willie, how are you? How's Atalanta?"

"Aphrodite."

"Sorry, Aphrodite, of course."

"She's pregnant, Buddy. I had you on my list to call and brag about it."

"Wonderful! How far along is she?"

"Six months. I think."

"Ah."

"How are you? How's Kalma?"

"Oh, sure, ok. Yes, she's ok."

"Honeymoon go well?"

"Uh, yeah. Sure. Went great. Beautiful beaches, good food."

"What's up, Buddy?"

"I want to talk about poetry."

"Sorry?"

"Poetry. The writing of."

"Ok. I've never tried it but I hear it's a hard game."

"Yes, I'm finding it so. But, listen. I have about 25—or 27—finished poems. What do I do with them?"

"Hell, Billy, like I would know."

"I thought, from school, you know."

"Oh, well. Yeah. Lemme think."

"One of your professors."

"Yes. Dr. Howell, perhaps."

"Lincoln Howell?"

"Yes, you know him?"

"No, I don't. I saw his book in Burke's when I was shopping for poets to inspire me."

'You did that?"

"Is that farfetched?"

"No, of course not."

"His book, um, *The Tumble Away from Distraction*. Is it good?"

"I think it's *Stumble Away*. Yes, from what I remember, quite good. He's been published by all the big places. But, really, I am so far removed from that scene now."

"Is he still alive?"

"Oh. Yes, that is, I think so. He must be 90."

"How can I find him?'

And so, it was that a week later, after work one night, Billy found himself driving to a small house on the edge of Shelby Forest. It appeared to be the house of kehua and fairy folk, set against a backdrop of the forest primeval. In the gloaming, the house was a gingerbread house, and the wending sidewalk from the curb to the front door was so covered in leaves and branches it was clear no one had come that way in a while.

When the door opened after a five-minute wait Billy was shocked at what 90 looks like. Lincoln Howell was shaped like a question mark and his bald pate, which shone at one like a blank face, was surrounded by tendrils of dirty gray hair. He wore glasses the size of dog food cans and his clothes—jacket, vest, shirt—were food-specked. His liver spots had liver spots.

"Mr. Kos?" the old fellow spoke in a raspy susurration.

"Dr. Howell, I'm so happy you had time for me."

"Got nothing but time. Except I don't."

"Yessir."

"Willie said you'd bring me a little treat."

"Oh, yessir. Alabamie Blammie. Still so fresh it's oily."

"Delicious. Come in, come in. Forgive the mess. I assume it's a mess but I can't see very well. Sit if there is a place."

Billy sat on a piano bench, after he cleared it, in front of a piano so old its top had splintered and opened like an oyster. Instead of strings inside there were stacks of dusty books.

"The grass please."

"Yes, yessir. Here it is." Billy fished a small bag out of his pocket. Dr. Howell raised it up until it actually touched his thick glasses.

"Hmm, looks like good stuff. This calls for the old Tandyn Slave-master. Fire one up with me?"

"Certainly," Billy said.

"Would you like something to drink?"

"Yes, thank you, sir."

"I might have some old wine. Don't know. Old, old wine. I have Tang."

"Tang would be lovely," Billy said. He didn't know they still made Tang.

"I think I have orange or prune."

"Prune Tang," Billy said, without humor.

"Yes, or orange."

Dr. Howell shuffled away into a hallway dark as mourning weed. It was several minutes before Billy heard the shuffling start back his way. He'd apparently forgotten about the Tang.

"Here she is," the good doctor said. "I had forgotten I used it last in the bath."

The item in the professor's bony hands looked like the kind of bottle one might build a ship in. What it was was a cunning bong with dual tubes and an attached sterno burner underneath. It took a while but eventually there was a small bit of Blammie in the beaker and the contraption was ready for use.

"This takes two, so I'm happy to have a smoking partner tonight. Gets lonely out here in the woods, listening to the cries of the banshees and forest opinici. Ahh," Dr. Howell said as he set one end of a tube in his mouth. "Hop aboard!"

Billy took the other tube and was rewarded with a cool blast of boo that cleared his sensorium and erased his criminal record. It lit his brain and froze his scrotum. It read him Yeats and fed him 'Revolution #9.' It scrambled his eggs and smoked his bacon.

The two men were mostly quiet as they took turns on opposite ends of the Tandyn Slave-master. After a few well-placed blowgun blasts both smokers lay back on the couch cushions and let dreamland sing to them for a bit. *Ignis fatui* played across the walls like spirits of the dead. The house creaked like an old boat and, once or twice, Billy thought he heard voices from the Great Beyond, or at least the Pretty Good Beyond.

"Best dope I've smoked since Owsley's house," Dr. Howell said, finally.

"The Pooh character?" Billy asked.

"Bear," Dr. Howell answered.

The men were quiet again for a while.

"So, what brought you here, Billy? Something about poetry that's bothering you? You got poets in your attic? They're noisier than squirrels and harder to get rid of than ants."

"Yessir," Billy said. "Or, I mean no sir. I want to be a poet."

Dr. Howell snorted through his ancient nostrils.

"The pierian plague. Forgive me. But why the hell would you want to be a poet?"

"Lost love," Billy answered seriously.

"Ah," Dr. Howell said. Now he wrinkled his pre-wrinkled brows, knitted his unraveled wits, put all his years of experience into his answer. "I dig," he said.

"I didn't know I had poetry in me," Billy said, seriously again. "Perhaps I don't."

"Perhaps you don't," Dr. Howell half muttered. "Let's see what you got."

Billy looked for the envelope of typed sheets he'd brought in. Eventually, sometime a few hours later, he found them under his own ass.

"Sorry, here. They're kinda wrinkled."

"Poems should be wrinkled," Dr. Howell said. Billy could not tell if it was the pot or the poet speaking.

Dr. Howell put a pair of reading glasses over his already thick spectacles. The effect was somewhere between comic and steampunk. He put up a bone-like finger, signaling silence. Billy sat mum while his poetry was being scrutinized.

The old man looked up finally. He removed one pair of glasses, reached up to rub his eyes where his fingers met the second pair of glasses, which he then removed and rubbed his old encrusted eyes.

"How long have you been writing?" he asked.

"About six weeks," Billy said.

"Six weeks." Dr. Howell thought a bit, tapped the pages with one set of glasses and returned the other to his eyes. "You have before you a great future as a poet. You have written precociously and well and you have caught a whiff of the alchemist's brew. You will publish many books of poetry and you will write many fine poems. In other words, you are damned."

"Many books?" Billy hooted. "This is real? This is what you think?"

"It is. And I am a fair prognosticator."

"Dr. Howell, how can I thank you? This is the best news I've ever received."

"Bring me a little weed every once in a while, and we'll call it square."

"Yes, sir, I shall," Billy said. Shall? he asked himself.

But, the future was not quite as kind as this evening would seem to auger. Billy never got to visit the old poet again with a gift of weed. Lincoln Howell died a week later. The young prostitute he had hired called 911 (which still occasionally dispatched the aid needed) and then sat weeping next to his emaciated, papery, spotted and very dead body. She was also naked and did not seem to know it.

And Billy Kos was never to publish a single book of poems.

## CHAPTER TWENTY-SEVEN

Billy Kos returned home that night around 2 a.m. He was as stoned as the poor mook who gathered firewood on the Sabbath, and as happy as the stoners. As he slipped into his murky living room he was startled by a figure sitting on the couch, a gray outline near the moonlit window. The figure moved. It raised a spectral arm and turned on a lamp.

"Billy Kos, where were you all night?" Kalma asked. She sat there wrapped in a white sheet.

Billy Kos stopped and straightened his shoulders. "I was out," he said.

Kalma pulled her bottom lip. "I missed you," she said. Her bright eyes brimmed with tears.

This was unexpected. Billy had no defense prepared for such a salvo.

"Well, ok, Kalma," Billy said. He began to walk to his room, his precious sheaf of foolscap under his arm.

"Billy, wait," Kalma said. She was hesitant, unsure of herself.

"I'm tired," Billy said.

"Billy," Kalma then said. "Please. Look."

Billy turned like Lot's wife.

Kalma got to her feet and dropped the sheet. She was wearing nothing but her yellow panties. Her protuberant nipples caught the lamplight and made wicked shadows. She stood, legs akimbo, and Billy could not help but admire her solid columns.

"Mm hm," Billy said. "My."

At this Kalma brightened. "You still want your Kalma, don't you, Billy Kos? You still like this?" She seemed to be presenting her entire body as if a game show prize.

"Kalma," Billy said and exhaled. "Turn around slowly."

"Yes, Billy Kos." Kalma turned and when her back was to him she hesitated. She knew Billy could not resist her ass.

"Stop," Billy said. Kalma was now smiling toward the wall. She knew her Billy.

"A thumb in each side of the elastic band," Billy said.

Kalma had to think for a moment to understand, then she hooked her thumbs into the elastic above each hip. "Like this, Lover?"

"Yes," Billy said. "Lower them very slowly."

Kalma did. She was happy now. She was almost as happy as Billy. As her panties slid down to the floor she knew a power that was restorative.

"Uh huh," Billy said. "Bend over."

This was going better than Kalma had anticipated. She bent.

"Touch your toes. Spread your legs."

Kalma did. "You getting hard, Baby?"

"I am," Billy said. "Touch yourself."

Kalma did and sighed.

"Ok. Keep doing that," Billy Kos said.

Kalma was bringing herself off and began to make the sounds small animals make in their small animal games. She did not hear Billy leave. Nor did she hear him go to his bedroom and close the door and lock it.

## CHAPTER TWENTY-EIGHT

This was more like a declaration of war than a further frostiness. Kalma did not eat breakfast with Billy, nor did she eat dinner with him when he returned from the pot store. In fact, she did not come home until Billy had already gone to his room with Berryman's poems and a fresh legal pad. Billy heard her key in the lock. Heard her open the door and enter. Heard her throw down whatever had been in her hands onto the living room floor. Her old sloppiness had returned in spades. The house was beginning to look like a sty. Billy didn't care.

He put the pen nib to the paper. He relaxed his body and his mind. He began to hear the music of the spheres. He wrote one word and then another. And soon all outside distractions were gone.

Billy fell asleep with his Berryman open on his chest. He did not awaken until lemony sunshine was coming through his blinds. Billy picked up the Berryman, looked at the page he had read the night before. His head was too muzzy for Berryman's playful syntax. He picked up the legal pad and read the title he'd written there above sixteen squiggly lines. The title was "For my Wife, Who is Far Away."

Hm," Billy's little interior editor said.

But there was a bit he liked: "We were
the first lovers, waking in the woods, all
around us the world's ferity.
We were the first lovers."

Billy got out of bed, found his slippers next to the bed and shuffled them onto his cold feet. The air had a nip to it. He'd forgotten to check the thermostat before bed last night. As he exited his room he bumped into a man wearing a pink housecoat. The housecoat he recognized. The man he did not. He was young, perhaps 22 or 23 with a stubbly beard.

"Oops," he said. "Sorry, Captain."

"What—" Billy began and then Kalma came out of the kitchen.

"Rocket, this is my husband, Billy. Billy, my student, Rocket. We pulled an all-nighter."

The student snuffled a laugh into the sleeve of his pink housecoat.

"Sorry, Captain," he said again and stuck out a hand.

Billy looked at Kalma. Then he looked at Rocket.

"Good morning," Billy said, and floated into the kitchen to fix a bowl of Captain Crunch.

## CHAPTER TWENTY-NINE

At High on your Horse that day Billy was distracted by ugly thoughts. He wasn't as good as Kalma at this game, if game it was. The truth was that he still ached for Kalma. She had set up permanent residence in his libido and imagining another man between her otherworldly legs made Billy want to cry. Instead of crying he lit up a bowl of some new stuff Hamm had just brought in. Supposedly grown in Australia, in the manure from Koala bears, its mild hallucinogenic qualities were becoming the stuff of legend. This was the first batch to hit Memphis. Hamm called it The Allegory of Nick Cave.

"It's beautiful, man," Hamm said. "Do a bowl and your day will be pregnant with rainbows."

Billy smoked about a fingernail's worth and, at first, seemed to feel little in the way of comfort or diversion. Then a cloud of yellow genie smoke entered his thinker. "Hello, Spaceman," the little genie said.

Billy decided the day was going to be okay after all. The first customer through the door was dressed as The Walrus and Yoko Ono was by his side.

"Got any Mississippi Thunderfuck?" The Walrus asked.

"Of course," Billy said. "Lid?"

"Yes, please."

Billy went to the stockroom and returned with the lid in a neat paper sack with the store's logo printed on the outside.

"Anything else?"

"I don't think so," The Walrus said. "Carpenter?" he asked his partner.

Billy realized his mistake immediately. It could not be Yoko Ono for she had passed on. It was only The Carpenter. Billy hated The Carpenters.

"Nothing for me," The Carpenter said.

"Ok, nice of y'all to come in," Billy said.

The Walrus and The Carpenter turned to go and Billy had one more thought.

"I loved *A Spaniard in His Works*," he said with a goofy grin.

The Walrus turned. "We all did, Mate," he said.

Yes, this was shaping up into an okay day. Then Kalma's brother Arch came in. His little weaselly face was pinched into an unsightly smile.

"Billy Bob," he called out with false gusto.

"Hello, Arch," Billy said. The genie turned its back and began to knit a shroud.

"Whatcha got for yer brother-in-law, Billy Bob?"

"Anything we sell," Billy said.

"Sat right?" Arch said. He made a pretense of looking around. "Heard a little story about you, Bob. Heard a nasty story."

Billy made his mouth a minus sign.

"My sister is not too happy with her new husband. Right? Dad said I should drop in and see if there's anything I can do to, you know, bridge the gap. To be a, Whatcha callit?, peace envoy."

"It's not your business, Arch," Billy said. His voice was stuck in his throat. The elevator had stopped and the words leaked out over his 2nd floor lip.

"Oh, Billy Bob, that's where you're wrong. Family is my business. Dad says, Family is everything. We're very close, Bob, very close. So, I'm here to tell you, no more chippies. No more staying out all night. You will be there for Kalma 24/7, you got it?"

Billy looked at his brother-in-law. He saw no hope for his future with this clan. Though he loved his Kalma, he could not abide the two male members of the clan. And the enmity was mutual.

"I have no chippy," Billy thought to say. "Kalma is mistaken if she thinks I have taken another woman."

"Ok, Billy. Ok. That's what I'll tell Dad. If there is a return message I will be back to see you, right?"

And he was gone in a stink of sulfur.

## CHAPTER THIRTY

That evening Kalma and Billy found themselves home at the same time and so had dinner together. A sort of precarious truce took place in their small kitchen at the blond, wooden table Billy had eaten at every year of his life.

"Store busy today?" Kalma asked. She had made BLTs and slaw for dinner. The slaw had cashews in it.

"Busy enough," Billy said. He said it without spite and without feeling.

"I talked about the Jungian shadow to my class. Freshman class. I don't think they got it."

"Arch came into the store today."

"Oh, Arch," Kalma said. Did her voice betray foreknowledge of this?

"All but threatened me."

The two ate their sandwiches. Billy picked the cashews out of his slaw and ate them.

"There's one little freshman girl," Kalma said, after a while. "Cute as a pudding. I think all the boys want her. She sits in the front row and just smiles and smiles."

Billy waited for the denouement of the story. He waited in vain.

"We got some new stuff in," Billy said.

He did not elaborate either. It was a meal with two monologues.

But, for a few days, the truce lasted, and they ate breakfast and dinner together. The conversations never did catch fire. Evenings

Billy read and wrote. Kalma watched TV in her room, which used to be the master bedroom.

Having tried and abandoned Berryman's cracked style Billy had settled into a looser conversational style that owed something to William Carlos Williams and something to Lincoln Howell. Billy had returned to Burke's Book Store and bought the lone copy of Howell's book, *The Tumble Away from Distraction*. Billy thought it was pure gold. The sentences seemed to slither around on the page, changing direction like the Mad Mouse roller coaster, almost always with a stinger on their tails. Billy tried to digest Dr. Howell without emulating him too much. It was a strong pull and Billy fought it.

He had also picked up a 2nd hand copy of *Writer's Market 2020* and was making notes of possible places to send his poems. Some of the places were no longer extant. Some were too intimidating. Billy's idea was to start with the most welcoming ezines and journals, the ones which said, "newcomers welcome," or words to that effect.

One afternoon Billy had lunch with Willie, who had come into the shop for the new Australian weed.

"Be careful with this," Billy said, grinning like Allen Ginsberg.

"Right," Willie said. "Like don't smoke and fly an airplane."

"It'll give you righteous dreams," Billy said.

"Righteous," Willie replied.

Billy and Willie ate at Dumbo's, a new hotdog and hamburger place on the Highland Strip. Their specialty was putting unexpected things on hotdogs and hamburgers, but since that was their stated raison d'etre their clientele was hard to surprise and the chef was becoming more and more outrageous and the stress was beginning to show. Willie ordered the hamburger with marshmallow fluff and charcoal briquette scrapings. Billy had a hotdog with pickle relish and talcum powder.

"This is terrible," Billy said.

"Yeah mine is too. Inedible."

"Why do we eat here?"

"Everyone eats here."

'Yeah, that's right."

"So, tell me everything," Willie said. "How's it feel being rich? How's it feel selling pot for a living? How good is Kalma in the sack?"

"We're not rich. And I have moved out of Kalma's sack."

"What? Tell me it's not true."

"It's true. Willie, I, I don't know how much to tell you. I'm sure this is temporary."

"Of course," Willie said. "Everything is temporary. What went wrong?"

Billy took an absent-minded bite of his hotdog and spit it back out.

"I forgot it was awful for a moment."

Billy looked out the window onto Highland. There were students dressed in primary colors, pretty as lawn ornaments. The sun was glinting off the traffic. The hum registered just below the muzak which was either Eric Burdon or The Cuticles doing "House of the Rising Sun." Underneath it all the rumble of a locomotive coming from the west with fissionable material in large tank cars.

"Sex is like recreation for Kalma," Billy said finally.

"That's not too bad," Willie tried.

"It is if she thinks it's a team sport."

"She wants a threesome?" Willie said it so loud most of the lunchtime eaters, struggling with their own outré creations, turned toward them.

"No. At least I don't think so. She plays around with everyone. Everyone." Billy had a catch in his voice.

"I'm sorry, Billy. But, really, not everyone."

"Seemingly."

"Not me."

"Thank God for small favors."

"She sleeps around?"

"I suppose that's the phrase."

"What about you? Good for the goose?"

"Naw, I don't. I haven't."

"Might do you some good."

"I love Kalma. I love her."

"I know, man."

"What to do?"

"That I don't know."

"She's—feckless, amoral. I don't know."

"Feckless?"

"She—she seems beyond simple human honor. Maybe I'm feckless."

"No, you're pretty feckfull."

"Thanks, Willie."

And at home that night, the truce still in place, Billy almost spoke spoonily to Kalma, almost began to pitch woo like a young swain. Why didn't he? Because he could not decathect. Because it still broke his ever-loving heart that she was enjoying the company of other men.

## CHAPTER THIRTY-ONE

Billy heard about the passing of Lincoln Howell from a small squib in The Commercial USA Today, Memphis' daily paper. He called Willie.

"Did you see the CUSA today?" he began.

"I don't read that rag," Willie said.

"How do you get news?"

"Friends like you call. They always begin, Did you see the CUSA today? What's up?"

"Dr. Howell died."

"Oh damn. That's too bad. Though he was 137."

"But he had such a pure spirit."

"Pure spirit doesn't sound like a recipe for staying on this human plane."

"I guess not."

"Wanna go to the funeral?"

"No funeral. No family. They are cremating him the paper says."

"And doing what with the cremains?"

"I hate the word cremains."

"Me too."

"So, should we, like, see about taking the ashes?"

And that is how the ashes of Dr. Lincoln Howell found their way into Billy Kos's backpack and then onto a shelf in his childhood bedroom, right next to a Gumby and Pokey and a copy of *Abe Lincoln: Boy Rail-Splitter*.

Billy also was given his papers. There were about 975 unpublished poems. This was a responsibility Billy wished to bludge. Nevertheless, he began to go through them and put them in some kind of order. It seemed random at first—instinctual, perhaps—and then, suddenly, it made sense. In this way, Billy taught himself how to create a book of poems.

He tried the same thing with his own work, poems that also had never been published. He was still balking at sending stuff to literary journals. His own book did not seem as shapely. Yet there was a crude power to putting them in order, shuffling them and putting them in a new sequence. After two weeks of doing this he had a manuscript which he titled *Dreaming of My Father Leaving*. He also titled Dr. Howell's collection, which he had edited down to 525 poems, *Churching: The Uncollected Poems of Lincoln Howell.* He spent another week heavily annotating his copy of *Writer's Market*, eventually narrowing down his choices to New Directions and Lower Power Books. He sent a copy of each manuscript to these two presses.

And he felt hopeful.

Meanwhile, Kalma was around the house a lot. She never disturbed Billy when he was writing but their conversations at the dinner table were polite, overly polite. Billy seemed distracted. Kalma seemed like Kalma.

"Billy Kos, do you want to show me some of your poems?" she asked one night.

"Hm?"

"Your poems. Do you want to show me some?"

"Oh, no, no I guess not."

"I'd like to read them."

"They're not really for you," Billy said. He said it robotically and not intended to sting. It stung. Kalma pulled her lip. She knit her brows. Then she stood up and walked straight out the front door.

Billy smiled at her departure. "Kalma," he whispered.

While Billy had been in his room those many weeks Kalma was also taking little trips out into the world. Her student, Rocket Calamari, was mooning around after her. She treated him as if he were a loyal puppy.

Rocket lived in the dorm and it was dangerous for Kalma to go there to see him. Nevertheless, the night Billy told her the poems were not for her, she strode into the dormitory as if it were her kingdom. She found Rocket's room and rapped on the door. A drowsy-eyed blond woman opened the door.

"Mrs. Voyles," she said. She was wearing only a man's white dress shirt.

"Get lost," Kalma said.

"Wha?" the blond asked.

Kalma nudged the door open. Rocket was in his underwear trying to put a shirt on over his feet.

"Kal—Mrs. Voyles," he said, reddening. "What are you?"

"Rock?" the blond said.

"Uh, Sissy, I'll talk to you later, ok?"

"I don't know where my clothes are."

Kalma turned toward her and made with the Godzilla eyes. Sissy slipped out the door like a drift of smoke.

"She's cute," Kalma said.

"Yes, ma'am."

"Rock, she calls you. I like that."

"Kalma."

"Rock, stop putting that shirt on over your legs. Drop it!"

Rocket let go the shirt and straightened himself. "What are you doing here?"

"Inspection. Teacher's inspection."

"Really? Is that a real thing?"

"It is tonight."

"Ok," Rocket Calamari said. He sat on his bed.

"You got any fuel left in your rocket, Rock?" Kalma said.

Rocket laughed. "Is that why you're here?"

"Talk to me, Rocket Calamari," Kalma said, sitting next to him on the bed.

"I'm—you know, not much of a talker, I guess."

"Tell me a story and I'm yours," Kalma said. "I want literature. I want carnal poetry."

"Oh, God," Rocket said.

Kalma snuffled and started to rise.

"Ok, ok, wait," Rocket said. He actually put a finger to his forehead.

"Tell me the story of us, Rock."

"Of us. Yes. Yes, I see. Um, you are a great teacher."

Kalma said, "Yawn."

"Ok, wait. Ok. When you were my teacher you used to sit on your desk with your legs spread. It drove the male students wild, maybe even some of the female."

"Hm, hm."

"And I could not think about ids or superegos. All I could think about was what was behind those panties that were in such plain view. I wanted you so badly."

"So, what did you do?"

"I masturbated a lot."

"So then what did you do?"

"I stayed after class one day."

"That's right. Go on."

"I could barely talk because you were still sitting there and your legs were bare and they were all shiny and I wanted to see if they were as soft as they looked. So, I made up some bullshit about the psych paper I was supposed to be writing and told you I didn't really get Freud. And you said, 'You get it.' And time seemed to stop. You were looking right through me. And you were pulling your lip and it was so inviting I prayed that I was not mistaken and that you were really wanting me to make a move."

"Make a move," Kalma said, for no good reason. "What did I tell you I'd do?"

"You said that for some students you would do a little extra teaching."

"That's right." Kalma seemed to be remembering it for the first time during this story time.

"We went to your house. It made me really nervous. I didn't know your husband or if he was going to be there. I was scared to death. But you invited me in and gave me Kool-Aid and we went straight to your bedroom. I spilled the Kool-Aid."

"Yes, you did."

"I went to get something to clean it up and when I returned you had taken your dress off. You were the most beautiful thing I'd ever seen."

"That's it, Rock. That's the story. That's what I wanted to hear."

"And you said, why do they call you 'Rocket,' and I said the boys in middle-school gave me that nickname because I could come four times in one night. And you said, can you really do that? and I guess I said, yes, I can do that."

"Can you do that tonight?" Kalma asked.

"Four times?" Rocket asked.

"To start," Kalma said. "See what literature can do for us. You're already raring to go."

Kalma put her hand around Rocket's cock through his briefs. It was thick and knotty and Kalma wanted it. She wanted it because poems are hard to understand and because her husband did not appreciate her and because it felt good. Ultimately it was all about feeling good.

"I like your stomach muscles. Hm, they look nice. You play handball?"

"Yes, huh, ma'am."

"Did you have sexual relations with that little blond tonight?"

Rocket hesitated. He didn't want to talk. He wanted Kalma to keep holding his penis.

"Yes. Yes, ma'am. But she's not—"

"Stop. Don't care." Kalma was miles away from what her hand was doing. Kalma took her hand away.

"Do you want me to take it out? You said you love my dick."

"Hm? Oh, yes. I do. But my husband's is bigger. My husband has a really big dick."

Rocket was lost. He had no experience that taught him what to say and do. All he knew was right in the blood vessels around his glans. He only knew he wanted to fuck Kalma Voyles.

"Kalma," he said, his voice wee. "Can we get undressed?"

"Is Blondie gone for good?"

"I don't know."

"Doesn't matter. You want very badly to have sexual relations with me right now, don't you?"

"Yes. Yes, ma'am, I do."

Kalma raised her skirt slowly, inching the hem upward. It was her best trick. She knew her legs were the magic key.

Rocket Calamari let out an audible sigh as Kalma's panties came in view. He rose, as if impelled upward by angels, and pulled his own briefs off and stood before her naked. Kalma looked him over.

"I think I'm gonna go home now," she said. "Thank you for telling me that story."

## CHAPTER THIRTY-TWO

When Kalma got home there was still a crack of light under her husband's door. She crept up to it as if the room contained skittish feral kittens. She rapped lightly on the door.

She heard a movement within, the shuffling of papers.

"Yes?" Billy said.

"May I come in?" Kalma asked, her voice like polished silver.

"Yes, ok," Billy said.

Kalma entered the room and looked around. She smiled at the little-boyness of it, as if she didn't know the room. The space was different with Billy in it. She sat on the end of the bed and looked all around her husband's body, at the papers in his lap, at the books around him.

"What are you doing, Billy Kos?" she asked.

"I don't know," Billy said. He was peeved that his concentration had been broken.

"Are you writing poems?"

"Kalma, why are you here?"

"Hm, on Earth you mean? As in why did God make Kalma?"

"Kalma, I'm tired and in the middle of something. I apologize but I need to sleep soon."

Kalma now met her husband's eye.

"Billy Kos, I was wondering if you wanted to French kiss with me."

Billy expected anything but this. How to answer? He took a long time. He looked at the open door, which made him angry. He looked at the poems of William Carlos Williams, splayed like a shot bird next to him. He looked at the pad where he was writing. There was a sentence there with no ending. It was in search of a period. Any period. Alas, it would never find one and it would die on the vine.

"No," Billy Kos said.

Kalma's head jerked involuntarily. "Oh," she said.

"Sorry," Billy Kos said.

"Do you want to look at my legs then? I shaved them earlier."

"Kalma, I must finish this. Another time perhaps."

Kalma rose. She walked toward the open door. Billy watched her walk and tried not to think about her ass or her legs or her rickety heart which he loved with an unsurpassed ache. Kalma turned, started to say something, and then was gone. She left the door open.

Billy reluctantly moved his papers and books and got up and closed the door. Was there a poem there, a poem about an open door now closed? He didn't know. His head was befuddled and he was tired. He cleared his bed and turned out the light.

Sleep did not come for several hours. The inside of Billy's head tormented him with the subtle poison of indignity. When the alarm rang he could not say whether he had slept or not. And the poem that was interrupted shriveled like a worm caught in the morning sun.

## CHAPTER THIRTY-THREE

Weeks went by. The situation at home did not improve much. The times they sat at the kitchen table together were some of Billy's happiest moments. He imagined that the Kalma he thought he knew, the one he first fell in love with, would be returned to him because Billy believed that the world was just.

"How's the writing going?" Kalma asked one evening.

"Fine," Billy said.

"How's the store doing?" Kalma asked one morning.

"Fine," said Billy.

"How are your classes?" Billy asked one evening.

"I have some good students. I think they like me," Kalma said. She smiled one of her crooked smiles. Those smiles broke Billy's heart, over and over.

"They like those short dresses," Billy offered, without rancor.

"Billy Kos," Kalma said.

But she did not anger. Kalma rarely angered Billy realized. His wife, for all her quirky flaws, was not a hothead. Billy was the one with emotions running right under his thin skin.

At High on your Horse Billy began to get more responsibility and one afternoon Hamm asked him if he wanted to be assistant manager. A slight raise, more to do. Billy said of course he would and that he was very grateful.

"No need for gratitude," Hamm said. "You deserve it."

"Thank you, Hamm."

"Billy, have you seen my sister lately? She's asking about you. Bout every time I see her."

"I haven't," Billy said. "I've been so busy."

"You should call her sometime. Could you get a night away from the wife?"

"Oh, no, I don't know," Billy said. He was reluctant to lay out his marital difficulties and equally reluctant to admit that his time was taken up with writing poetry.

"Just a thought," Hamm said. "Her thought mostly."

This haunted Billy. He hadn't seen Rita since he rebuffed her advance on the same day she offered him this job. Did he remember where she lived? He did.

And, on the way home from work, he drove by her house, a little yellow bungalow on Tutwiler, not too far from the dairy. From his youth Billy remembered that driving by a girl's house never was very satisfactory. The idea that they might be standing outside under the porch light, lonely and horny, was absurd, of course, yet boys had been engaging in this ludicrous activity since the automobile was first used as an attractant. Edsel Ford cruised women's homes.

Billy remembered exactly which house was hers. And as he let the car roll slowly by there she was, Rita Someback, wondrous as a vision, out in her front yard, adjusting a lawn sprinkler. Billy's first impulse was to gun the car and get out of there fast. But he thought she would probably look up and recognize the car. So, he braked. His car sat in the middle of the road. A car behind him honked and swerved around him, the driver's angry expression passing like a dark swirl.

Rita Someback looked up. She put her hand up to her pretty eyes, shading them, and blew a light blond tendril out of her face. Her smile was as pretty as a pippin. She was wearing a man's checkered shirt with the sleeves rolled up and ridiculously small and tight blue jean shorts.

"Hey Billy," she called out.

Billy maneuvered the car to the curb and got out.

"Hi Rita," Billy said, pocketing his keys and bumping his shin on the fender of the car.

"Smooth as ever," Rita said and laughed her laugh, which was like a jack-in-the-box falling down a wooden staircase.

"That's me," Billy riposted.

"Remember the time in Mrs. Reid's class when you broke the prop sword."

Billy wrinkled his face. "I don't," he said.

"Billy. Remember the cardboard castle we built to stage Macbeth?"

"Jeez, I don't think I do."

"Billy Kos. Remember our first kiss?" Rita said and let another laugh tumble out.

"In the dugout. You slugged me."

"I did," Rita said, her laughs eking out still.

"Not just our first kiss, but our only," Billy said. It came out as more of a taunt than he meant.

"Come here, Buddy," Rita said, blowing another tendril off her sweaty brow, and grabbing the front of Billy's shirt. She pulled his face downward and placed her lips directly over his, planting her tongue in his mouth and letting it squeegee around a bit.

"Oof," Billy said, when she let him go.

"Now, I have officially apologized for that punch. You wanna come in?"

"Rita, it would be my fondest dream."

So, they found themselves on Rita's couch again and the talk was easy and free and they were sipping white wine and telling high school stories and moving closer and closer to each other.

They kissed again. This time it lasted a good long time. It was tender and affectionate and it lasted a long time. Stars were born and died.

Billy was aroused. He felt like he felt in high school. He wanted to touch Rita Someback's breasts. And then he did. His hand palmed her left breast and she exhaled into his mouth.

"Billy," she said, disengaging. She laid her head on his chest and put a hand inside his shirt. He kept gently kneading her perfectly round breast. Its nipple rose between his fingers. He let it go and began to undo the buttons on her shirt. When it was open there was a flesh-colored bra in his way. He slipped his hand around her back and unsnapped the clasp with two fingers.

"Well-done," Rita said, now massaging Billy's stomach under his shirt.

Her breasts were as lovely as he had anticipated. They were moonlight and velvet. He began to play with them. Their heft in his hand was a remarkable thing. And Rita began to breathe a little heavier. Her hand undid Billy's belt. His cock was straining at the front of his pants and he wanted nothing more than that she should release it.

She did. It sprang upwards like a plaything.

"Billy," Rita said.

"Oh, Rita," Billy said.

"You're so big," Rita said.

"Oh, Rita," Billy said. "Am I? Kalma says so."

Billy almost killed the buzz. Rita persevered.

Rita traced a finger around his pubic hair, over his testicles lightly. Then up the vein in his shaft. Then she closed it in her soft fist.

"If I had known," she whispered. She began to lower her head toward him and something terrible happened. Billy went soft. He deflated and all but receded into his body. Rita stopped, then started toward him again, her mouth now the medicine needed.

"Rita," Billy said.

"What? What happened?"

"I can't do it," Billy said. He seemed near tears.

"Do you have a problem, Billy dear? Do you want to talk about it?"

Rita backed up. Her shirt remained open but Billy pulled his pants back over his shame.

"The problem is that I love my wife," Billy said into his own chest.

Rita had not expected that. She sat back and pulled her shirt together with one hand.

"I see," she said. Her feelings were hurt but she tried to rally and be supportive.

"I'm sorry. Again, I'm sorry," Billy said. He stood and did up his pants and rebuckled his belt.

"Billy, I, I'm not sure that this isn't all my fault. I'm the one who is sorry. I've been wanting to do this with you for a long time. I supposed Hamm told you to come by."

"No," Billy lied. Well, he certainly hadn't told him to come by. He had only cracked the door.

"I best go home," Billy said. "I'll be late for supper."

At the door they kissed one more time. It was a nice kiss. It was as warm as a cutlass blade.

## CHAPTER THIRTY-FOUR

And then Kalma disappeared for three days.

At the end of the second day Billy thought about calling the police. He was sure they would view it as a domestic situation and perhaps castigate him for not controlling his woman.

At the end of the third day Billy called Boils Voyles at his home landline, which the Voyles family kept so the servants could answer it. After a servant, whose voice Billy did not recognize, answered, Billy asked for Mr. Voyles.

"Hello, Billy," the father said.

"Listen, I am concerned about Kalma."

"Concerned, are you?"

"Yes, sir."

"Sick is she?"

"No, sir. That is, I don't think so."

"You don't think so?"

This was going off the rails quickly.

"Mr. Voyles, do you know where Kalma is?" Billy said in exasperation.

"Yes, I do, Billy. She is here."

"May I speak to her, please?"

"I'll see if she would like to speak to you."

Billy held for a long time.

"Hello, husband," Kalma said.

"Jesus, Kalma, what are you doing?"

"What do you mean, Billy Kos?"

"You didn't even leave me a note to say where you are. Didn't you think I'd be concerned?"

"Hm," Kalma said. "I think I meant to leave a note."

"Come home please."

"Billy Kos, I am home. I am at my original home."

"Kalma, are you leaving me?"

There was a silence that was as long as the passage of numberless ages in slumberless song and as cruel as dust.

"I guess not," Kalma said.

"Are you coming home now, then?"

"I can do that, Billy."

"Why did you leave, Kalma? I love you."

This silence was neither as pronounced nor as incogitant.

"I love you, too, Billy Kos," Kalma said.

And so she came back home. And that night they slept in the same bed. It was a cold bed. It was not the marriage bed. It was more like the bed at the bottom of the ocean. It was not procrustean but it wasn't anticrustean, either. They did not touch except for a kiss before sleep. But they were together, sleeping together, like before, almost. Almost like before.

In the morning Kalma began to tell Billy about her three days away.

## CHAPTER THIRTY-FIVE

The next day's breakfast was as joyful a meal as Billy had enjoyed in some time. Their conversation had a warmth to it that had been missing, that Billy had sorely missed. He had been called back from his island, if only temporarily. He felt rescued.

"These are tasty pastries. What are they?"

"Scones," Kalma said, standing in a puddle of raw dough and wiping flour from her freckled nose.

"With some kind of meat in them?"

"Kidneys. I used kidneys."

Billy paused. "They're kidney scones."

Kalma looked up and smiled. "They're good with Kool-Aid," she said. "But I also love this orange juice. Smack, smack," Kalma said.

"Mm," Billy answered with a smile.

"Who first thought of that, do you wonder? Squeezing fruit?"

"I don't know. The beatinest person, I imagine."

"Yes."

"Kalma, I missed you."

"I missed you, too, Husband."

"Why did you leave?"

"Well, I didn't really plan to leave. I didn't pack a bag or anything. I just went to visit my father because you didn't come straight home from work."

"I was having an after-work toke with Hamm."

"Oh, that's nice."

"So, you went to your father's and he persuaded you to stay there?"

"No, Billy Kos. My father didn't persuade me."

"So why did you stay so long?"

"Tomboy persuaded me."

Billy's breakfast began to trace its route back upward.

"Tomboy," Billy choked out.

"Yes. You know Tomboy."

"Of course I know Tomboy. Why did he persuade you to stay there?"

"Well, you know, Billy Kos. You know about me and Tomboy."

"I—I don't think I do."

Kalma hummed and looked around. She read the back of the Captain Crunch box. There was a puzzle there and Kalma began to try and solve it. It had something to do with getting to the pirates' loot.

"Oh," Kalma said. "Did you see this mail? Something from a book publisher."

She reached the counter behind her and the mail that came yesterday had not been opened. In between a Victoria's Secret catalog and a Kroger coupon booklet were two envelopes. One was from New Directions and the other from Lower Power Books. In his despair at missing his wife the day before Billy had not even examined the mail.

He opened the New Directions envelope first. It was a boilerplate rejection of his manuscript. It said, "We are not sufficiently in love with this book to publish it." It was written by a robot.

In the envelope from Lower Power Books there were two separate sheets of paper. One was an acceptance of Lincoln Howell's previously uncollected poems. It asked if Billy was his agent or heir?

The other was an acceptance of Billy's own book, *Dreaming of My Father Leaving*. It praised the manuscript's wit and depth. It praised its cockeyed and idiosyncratic non-style. It praised its movement from light to dark to light again. Billy had to read it through twice. He set it down on the table. A tear ran from one eye. It was probably his left eye.

"What is it, Billy Kos? Did they reject your poems?"

"What? Yes," Billy Kos said. "One did."

He was staring at his wife but he was not seeing her.

"One did," she repeated. "I'm sorry, Husband."

"And then one didn't," Billy finished.

"What? What do you mean?"

"Lower Power Books wants to publish my book of poems."

Kalma stood up and put her arms around Billy. Billy stood, awkwardly because shackled by her arms, and then put his arms around her. He kissed her deeply. His passion was red hot.

"Billy Kos," Kalma said, when they broke the kiss. "You should get accepted more. I forgot what a good kisser you are. I like French kissing."

"I know you do, Wife," Billy Kos said. And then he let the tears come from both eyes.

"Whoo-hoo, I wish I didn't have class this morning," Kalma said. She patted her husband on the ass.

"Tonight, we celebrate," Billy said.

"Yes, let's. Can we have Yoohoos?"

"Of course we can," Billy said, laughing.

"And don't forget how to French kiss."

## CHAPTER THIRTY-SIX

Billy was very close to ecstatic, right next door to ecstatic, no fence or guard dog. Even though he knew nothing of how publishing worked he assumed he was on his way.

"I'm on my way," he told Hamm at work. "You've heard of Lower Power Books, of course."

"I haven't, Billy, but I don't read much."

"Uh huh. You know, they published Gordon Osing, Agile Implaw, Pope Clerk. . ."

"I don't—"

"Katey Cook! You've heard of Katey Cook!"

"She's on *You are a Candidate*, right?"

"No, she's not a TV star. You know, 'Fireworks in the Gorge,' 'Jack-leg Holiday,' 'My Medicine is Making Me Sick'."

"These are—what? Songs?"

"Hamm, they're poems. Very famous poems."

"And they'll be in the same book as you?"

Billy stared at his boss. He was up against something but he did not know what yet. "Never mind. It's not important. I have a book coming out. That's all."

"Hey, I'll come to your signing. Have you called Burke's?"

"A little premature probably."

"Right. Sure. Want me to call for you?"

The rest of the day was taken up with the quotidian aggregate of stoners, hipsters, addicts and cancer patients. He tried to talk to one willowy young woman with an opossum tattooed on her arm, tried to shoehorn his news into a casual conversation, but she wasn't having it. Her bushbaby eyes said, *just gimme my dope, Dope.*

By the time he got home Kalma already had a meal on the table. It was grits with hotdogs cut up in them, green beans, lime jello with lentils, and sweet potatoes with ice cream for dessert. The sweet potatoes were raw.

"My wife," Billy said, affectionately.

"I'm so happy tonight, Billy Kos."

"You're sweet, my wife. I love you."

"I love you, too, Poot. I mean, poet. My poet."

"Yes."

"Now you will let me read some poems."

"Always. Forever and always."

They ate slowly, with demonstrative gestures and kindly smiles. Kalma kept petting Billy's forearm as if it were a ferret. Once Billy looked up from his grits to find her staring intensely at him. She held his gaze and licked her puffy lips. Billy got an erection. He was hoping to skip those rigid yams and hop into the connubial sack instead.

"All this news, Billy Kos," Kalma said, dreamily as they approached the end of the main course. "All this change."

"Yes, my love," Billy said.

"Billy. Maybe I should tell you this now."

Billy felt a flip in his stomach as if an imp inside him had just rolled dice that came up snake eyes.

"Is it something bad, Kalma?" Billy said, timorously.

"No, I don't think so. I really don't."

"Tell me quickly."

"I started to tell you about being at my old home. Where was I? Oh, well, you know, Tomboy?"

Billy nodded. His mouth was sere. Serer than sere.

"He wanted me to stay there. I told him, Tomboy, I love you, but I am married to Billy Kos."

"I don't understand. Why would—the *help* ask you to stay there?"

Kalma hummed a bit. She tapped her fork on the table.

"It went like this." She took a deep breath. "Tomboy and I were in my bed."

"What? What—the hell do you mean?"

"Billy Kos, I told you. Tomboy and I were practically raised together. We played together as children. He taught me everything. He taught me how to French kiss. You know how good I am at French kissing."

Billy was dumb. He was lost.

"We were in my bed. You know it's not true about them all having bigger dicks. I told Tomboy that. I told him that my husband has a bigger dick. He was quite surprised. But then Tomboy's dick is the one I've known longest. You know. Since he taught me all about sex and that kind of thing. The first time he told me to put his dick in my mouth I thought he was kidding." Here Kalma laughed. Billy almost hit her with his dinner plate.

"Kalma—I can't believe what I'm hearing. You—you've been with him all along?"

"I don't know what you mean."

"Wait, wait," Billy said. "When we first got together you told me you'd never done oral sex before."

"Well, Billy, it's more exciting that way, isn't it? Like you're teaching me. I thought you needed to hear that, to do it that way."

"Fuck. Forget it. Finish this damn story."

"Oh, you're pissy now."

Billy made a gesture. It was incoherent.

"Anyway, we were completely naked and, since Dadsy keeps it so hot in that house, we were on top of the covers and it was afternoon so I could see everything pretty well and that's when I told Tomboy about your dick being bigger, though when you put them in your mouth they feel about the same size if you know what I mean. And so, Tomboy said that size doesn't matter and it was duration that counted and so we talked about that for a while and then he wanted to do it doggy style—he always wants to do it doggy style—and I said, Ok Tomboy. Let me wiggle my ass for you. And then I told him the other news."

Billy opened his mouth. No sound came out. His eyes were watering, perhaps drawing all moisture from his oral cavity.

'The. Other. News," he managed.

"That I'm pregnant. I know, it's surprising to you. It surprised Tomboy, too. Well, it surprised me too, believe me. I was hoping that you wouldn't care, you know, whose child it is, since we're married and you're my husband and I don't want anything to change that and I told Tomboy that. I told him that flat out."

"Whose," Billy said. It rhymed with noose.

"Well, of course, it's probably Tomboy's because you and I always use the sponge."

Billy sat stock still. He knew if he moved the movement might kill his wife. He knew that he was capable of picking up an eating utensil and placing it between her eyes. He feared to move even one finger.

"It'll be a pretty baby, Billy. You'll love him or her. Little milk chocolate colored baby. You've seen little mulatto pickaninnies? So cute. And we will be happy the three of us, of that I am sure."

"Kalma," Billy said, calmly. "If I move even one finger I will kill you. I will kill you until you are dead."

Kalma moved back as if slapped.

"Billy Kos," she said, "You wouldn't hurt me."

Billy stared. Then he felt the blood return to his extremities. He could move. He could stand up. Before he did he said, plainly, "So you fuck him without protection."

"Tomboy says the spermicide tastes funny and the sponge hurts his head." Kalma smiled a skewwhiff smile.

"I see," Billy said.

"I told him you never complained and that doesn't make good sense to me because, you know, your dick is bigger, which I would think would cause you discomfort, but, anyway, it's just old Tomboy so I wanted to keep it all friendly and all. He'd never made me pregnant before. That's odd, isn't it?"

"I see," Billy said.

And then Billy rose and went to his room. Once there he packed up his papers in one small valise and some clothes in another and he calmly walked out of his childhood home forever.

"Billy Kos, I'm sorry if it made you mad," Kalma said as he drifted by. "It's just sex, Billy and I just think. . ."

Her words grew fainter and fainter, dopplering away like a train going, going, going—moving inexorably toward the endgame, a derailing, a crash, a sweet-visaged death.

## CHAPTER THIRTY-SEVEN

And so, Billy ran. Not literally but figuratively. He got in his car and ran. His first impulse was to go to Rita's but that seemed crazed. What woman would want such a man?

He knocked on Willie's door. The night had begun to produce rain and the rain ran down Billy's face, matching, drop for drop, the tears which Billy was vaguely aware he was shedding. He could feel it in his chest more acutely, a pain like surgery, as if his pump organ were being were being played by Old Scratch.

"Billy, what the hell?" Willie said.

"Who is it?" Aphrodite shouted from the interior. Her stridulant voice sounded like a sick foghorn.

"It's Billy. Something's wrong," Willie shouted back. Billy stood in the rain.

"Can I come in?"

"Sorry, of course. What happened?"

"Kal-Kal-Kal," Billy said. He stumbled toward the couch and dropped onto it, dripping onto its horrible, artificial surface.

"Lemme get you a drink," Willie said. He passed his wife as she came into the room with a quizzical expression. Willie shrugged as he passed her.

"Hello, Billy," Aphrodite said. She stood against the far wall as if what Billy suffered from was contagious.

"Af-Af-Af," Billy said.

"Be calm," Aphrodite said.

"I'm s-sorry," Billy said. "I'm, I'm fucked."

"It is possible to know about the mind, the spirit and life," Aphrodite said.

Willie re-entered the room with a tumbler of something brown in his hand.

"Af, Billy doesn't need Scientology right now."

Aphrodite opened her mouth to refute, thought about it, and left.

"Sorry," Willie said. He handed Billy the drink. Billy swallowed a small portion.

"What is this?" he asked.

"I'm not sure. Aphrodite peels the labels off. She objects to my drinking so she makes it hard on me."

"It's awful."

"I know what it is then."

They were quiet for a few moments except for Billy's blubbering into his own lap. When he looked up at his friend his eyes were hollow. He was hollow. Inside he was air, wind, forfeiture.

"Did Kalma leave you?" Willie asked.

"W-why would you assume that's the problem?" Billy asked.

"I don't know. Billy, I don't know anything. Tell me what's going on."

"Kalma. Kalma," Billy said.

Willie waited. He took the glass back from Billy and put it on the coffee table.

"Kalma is pregnant." That seemed to be the heart of the matter.

Willie waited some more. That couldn't be the problem.

"It's not mine," Billy said.

And they got down to it. Billy laid it all out for his friend. Willie did not interrupt once until Billy finished, spent, his chest now heaving with dry sobs.

"She doesn't think sex is, um, exclusive. Even between husband and wife." It seemed a nonsensical thing to say but its literalness hit the spot.

"Yes," Billy said. "That's it. I've been kidding myself. All this time I tried to ignore what I thought were just her quirky ways, her *innocence*, for God's sake."

"I like Kalma," Willie started.

"I don't want to hear that," Billy said.

"Listen. She's always been an odd bird. And, well, I saw her kissing that black guy at the wedding."

Billy looked up. "I saw that too. They always kissed like that. I tried to tell myself that I was just uptight and that I should try to be more like her and her family, easygoing about sexuality. But, Willie, Goddamit, all this time—"

"I know, Buddy. You wanna stay here we've got the extra room."

"Thanks, Willie."

"Are you hungry?"

"No, I just want to go to sleep. You got anything?

"Lots of pot."

"Yeah, I packed some pot."

"Quaaludes."

"Where did you get them? I haven't seen ludes in years."

"Vintage shop on Cooper."

So, though Billy could not sleep that night until dawn was already cracking its rosy knuckles, thus began Billy's bunking at Willie and Aphrodite's. Kalma called once but Aphrodite denied all knowledge of Billy's whereabouts. Willie had called Hamm and told him what was going on and Billy was given all the leeway he needed.

After a week, Billy attempted re-entry to the world. He went to work and after work he went to Rita's for dinner.

## CHAPTER THIRTY-EIGHT

"Come in, Billy," Rita said. She was wearing something simple, a one-piece dress of a muted flower pattern, but her body made it appear a living thing, a burrower, a fire, succor.

"Something smells good," Billy said. His voice was low, full of breath as if he'd run there.

"I'm not much of a cook," Rita said. "Do you like wine before dinner?"

"I don't know. Yes," Billy said.

"It's got a few more minutes," Rita said, handing Billy a flute of white wine and sitting next to him on the sofa. The living room opened onto the kitchen. It was almost one big room.

"How are you doing?" Rita said. Her eyes crinkled at the edges when she squinted in sympathy, sipping her wine.

"I'm ok," Billy said.

"I know," Rita said. She was nervous. They were quiet for a while.

"Is it spaghetti?" Billy asked.

"Oh, no. Lasagna. Do you like lasagna?"

"I think yes. Yes, I like lasagna."

Rita smiled, sipped. So far Billy had not lifted his flute as if it would be a lot of work to bring it all the way to his mouth.

"Lemme take that," Rita said. She took the glass from Billy's hand, which Billy released without volition. Rita set both glasses on the coffee table.

"Come here," Rita said. "We're both nervous."

She put her arms around Billy and Billy leaned into her. She smelled like something good, flowers or cookies. Billy breathed her in. She held him until a timer went off.

"Lemme get that," Rita said, leaving Billy on the couch. "It should sit for a moment. Maybe I'll see about the garlic bread while it rests."

The dinner was delicious, Billy thought, spooning smaller and smaller bits into his mouth. He had not had much of an appetite of late. He was losing weight and he wasn't sleeping well. He was sure he looked a fright.

After dinner Billy offered to do the dishes.

"Let's leave them to soak," Rita said.

They returned to the couch.

"Do you want to watch TV? Or a movie?" Rita asked.

"I don't know, sure."

"We can just talk," Rita said, as if it had been voted on. "Do you want to take your shoes off?"

Billy looked at his shoes. He reached down and untied them and slipped them off, gently pushing them under the coffee table. Rita took hers off. Her bare legs, ending now in bare feet, seemed particularly beautiful, shiny as new cookware. She tucked them under herself and settled down very close to Billy.

After silence became awkward Rita spoke Billy's name quietly and when he turned she placed her lips against his. Billy kissed back. It felt good. It felt right. Rita warmed to it and Billy responded.

She unbuttoned Billy's shirt and ran her hand lightly around his chest. Billy raised one hand. Once he did he had to do something constructive with it so he placed it over her breast. Rita exhaled a lovely exhale.

They did that for a while. Then Rita undid Billy's belt. Billy helped her lower his trousers and then helped her lift her dress over her head. Rita undid her own bra and her breasts were rosy and her nipples sharp little nuggets. Billy wanted to suck there and so he did.

Rita began to pant. "Billy," she said. "Oh, Billy."

Billy was feeling pretty good. When Rita reached into his underwear and pulled out his cock everything seemed to be going swimmingly. He tugged at her panties and, together, they managed to get them.

"Billy, you've got such a great dick," Rita said. She wrapped it almost reverently.

"Ah, ah," Billy said. Relief came to his subconscious. This was going to work.

"I'm so wet already," Rita said and she swung one leg over him. As she lowered herself over him she whispered, "I'm on the pill."

Then it all went pear-shaped. Billy's erection liquesced. Rita reached under herself and tried to knead it back into shape. She juggled his balls, pulled on his tommy. It only shrunk further. Rita was rubbing its nub into her wetness when Billy began to sob.

"I'm sorry," he said. "Some great date."

"Hush," Rita said.

She dehorsed and sat naked beside him. She pulled his head onto her chest. Billy wept silently for a while.

"Would you like to sleep here tonight?" Rita asked after a while.

"I don't know. Yes," Billy said.

And so, they slept together. And Billy slept well.

In the morning Rita tried to wake Billy by felating his piss-erection. Billy woke, saw Rita's beautiful backside bent over him and began to cry again.

The next night they went out to eat. They returned to Rita's and went to bed together. Rita wore skimpy, see-through wisps of lingerie which made Billy's cock rock hard. But, again, he could not follow through. He was losing faith in himself as a man.

The next night went similarly. Rita suggested they shower together. No good. The night after that they only slept together, kissing a bit before giving in to Morpheus. A few nights later Rita tried one more time to get Billy inside her. The harder she tried the spongier Billy became. Now he couldn't even get it up during foreplay.

"Billy," Rita said, one night over dinner at her place. "You can get help, you know? If you want to, if it's important to you."

"Important to make love with you?" he asked.

"Not exactly that," Rita said, playing with the veins on the back of Billy's hand. "To help you forget. To get you past Kalma."

"I know. But shrinks are expensive and that could take years. I'm dead, Rita. I'm sorry you had to hook up with me. I am dead now and nothing will bring me back."

"Codswallop."

"I'm very, very fond of you, you know. You're the loveliest woman."

"But until you get past Kalma no woman is going to be good for you."

"I guess that's true."

"So, listen. I've been reading on the net about this new technique. It's called Disremembering. You can be programmed to be like you were before whatever trauma is blocking you. You can literally become the man you were before Kalma."

Billy looked at her with cow eyes.

"I was a child."

"You were a happy child. It's still in you to be that happy child again. It's supposedly painless. It involves a form of time travel."

"Time travel? That sounds, forgive me, ridiculous."

"It does, I know. I've read a lot about it. It's really helped some people. Memphis has a clinic, too. In Southaven, in what used to be Graceland."

"In Elvis's house?"

"Yes. After it went belly-up it was repurposed as a Disremembering Clinic. They do other things like with sensory deprivation tanks and Altered States kinds of things but this Disremembering is really catching on. Can I make you an appointment?"

## CHAPTER THIRTY-NINE

The next morning Billy called Kalma. She was having breakfast before heading out to school.

"Good morning, Billy Kos," she said.

"Kalma," Billy said.

"Do you want some breakfast?"

Billy hesitated. "Maybe. Are you going to teach today?"

"Yes, Billy, I am going to teach today."

"Can we talk?"

"Of course, Billy Kos."

"I mean in person. Can I come over?"

"I won't have time unless I don't teach my first class."

"Can you do that? Skip your class?"

"No, I don't think so. It's my best class."

"Kalma, I want to talk about us. I want to give it a chance."

"Hm, hm, Billy. I don't think so now. I tried to call you."

"I know. I'm sorry." He was apologizing.

"Tomboy lives here now."

Billy was sure he hadn't heard right. "What?" he said.

"Tomboy moved in with me. He's sleeping with me in our old room. I tried to call you to ask you if it was okay."

"If—it—was—okay," Billy croaked. "Kalma."

"I didn't think you wanted Kalma anymore."

"Kalma," Billy croaked.

"I'm sorry, Billy. Is that all?"

It was all. Billy had nothing left. He was used up. He was spent. "That's everything," he said.

That night he asked Rita to make an appointment with Disremembering for him.

"Of course, I will," Rita said. She put a hand on his cheek.

"I had to know for sure it was over."

"What is over, Billy?"
Billy looked at Rita Someback. Her face flickered with kindness.

"Nothing. I want to be whole for you, Rita. You are dear to me."

"Billy Kos, what a sweet thing to hear. You are dear to me, also."

"I will erase Kalma and you and I will be together. I want you, Rita."

"Oh, Billy." Rita kissed Billy for a long time.

"And we will be together and I will be a published poet and it will all be good."

"A published poet?"

"You don't even know. I had my book of poems accepted by Lower Power Books."

"Billy, that's wonderful. They're good, Lower Power, aren't they?"

"Yes. They are good."

"When is it coming out?"

"I don't even know. But I will find out. Wait."

"What is it, Darling?"

She called me darling, Billy Kos said to Billy Kos. "Will I not remember you or the book or how to write poems? I don't want total amnesia."

"No, it's very specific. I don't understand it all. It's based on physics, on something called time dilation. We can ask when we're there."

"Are you going with me?"

"If you'd like."

"I would, Rita. Beautiful Rita."

"Handsome Billy."

Billy had never been called handsome before. Did Rita love Billy? Did Billy love Rita? Suddenly Billy had a new future. He wanted to move into it.

## CHAPTER FORTY

The musical gates of Graceland were wide open and the front lawn had been paved for parking. Inside the front door was a receptionist's desk. The interior was completely transformed. It now looked like a tony sanitarium.

"Good morning," the pretty receptionist said.

"Billy Kos," Billy Kos said.

"Of course, Mr. Kos. If you'll turn to your immediate right and find a seat you will be given a couple forms to fill out."

"Thank you," Billy said. "Is it ok if Rita comes with me?"

"Of course. She'll have to wait outside during the procedure, though."

"Thank you," Billy said again.

The forms were extensive and it took Billy almost thirty minutes to complete them. Rita scanned the magazines on the rack. *Time* and *Newsweek*. *Good Housekeeping*. And ex-President Trump's publication *Pussy Galore*. Rita decided to play games on her phone instead.

"All done?" a woman was standing in front of them. She was wide and had a head of Harpo hair and she was smiling like a May morning.

"Y-yes," Billy said. He was nervous. Rita took his hand and squeezed it.

"Dr. Lightman is ready. May I take you to him?"

"Thank you," Billy said. He looked at Rita and she kissed him quickly on the lips.

"See you soon, Love," Rita said.

She loves me, Billy Kos said to Billy Kos.

The room he was taken to was small and sterile. Everything was white except for a silver metallic box about the size of a hotel room refrigerator. There were myriad wires and devices hanging from it and beside it a comfortable chair something like an antiseptic Lazy-Boy.

Dr. Lightman was a small, compact man about 60 years old. He had a boyish face and a puckish grin.

"Hello, Billy," he said.

"Dr. Lightman," Billy said.

"You're nervous."

"Yes, I am."

"Let me put you at ease. You've read up on our procedure. What aspect of it frightens you?"

"I'm a writer."

Dr. Lightman waited. "And this affects us how?"

"I don't want to lose the part of me that writes. I don't want to forget that I am a poet and that I have a book coming out. And, um, I don't want to forget Rita."

"This is your wife?"

Billy hesitated. "No, sir. Rita is waiting for me outside. My wife is who I want to forget." "I see. And you are divorcing?"

"Oh. No," Billy said.

"Usually the divorce comes first."

"I can't wait that long," Billy said. His earnestness touched Dr. Lightman.

"Ok, then. Let me explain a few things. I don't imagine you're familiar with retrocausality?"

"Um, I don't think so."

"Well, simply put, there is a causal loop which allows us to stick pins in the wave motion of time itself. You will be temporarily, if we can use that term, atemporal."

Billy grinned. If this were the idea simply-put he didn't care about its complexities. He stopped listening though the doctor went on and on.

"So, you will lose the part you have chosen to lose and the rest remains, in a manner of speaking, still in your loop."

"I'm sorry. What was that last part?"

Dr. Lightman repeated his last few sentences.

"Ok, I'm convinced," Billy said. "How long does it take?"

"Time being fluid."

"Yes."

"No time at all." Dr. Lightman smiled. Billy assumed this was an egghead joke. Dr. Lightman put a reassuring hand on Billy's shoulder. "Let's get started," he said.

The wide-hipped, Harpo-haired assistant woman came in. Was she a nurse? Is this a medical procedure, Billy thought for the first time? Billy was hooked up to the mini-fridge by numerous wires and connectors. Some lightly penetrated his epidermis, some were held in place by some form of medical epoxy. Billy watched with fascination.

"Now, you will sleep briefly because we have found the process at first is a bit disorienting. When you wake the pain Kalma caused will be a thing of the past. Your pain, in essence, will be forgotten. Ok?"

Billy grinned his approval and then he was put under.

Dr. Lightman and his assistant checked all contacts. The doctor fiddled with the machine, using its data entry keyboard and its power levels to set up the proper sequencing. The machine began to hum. The lights in the room flickered. Dr. Lightman and his assistant felt a pain shoot through their cerebrums. The lights went out and a few seconds later came back on.

"Uh oh," Dr. Lightman said.

## CHAPTER FORTY-ONE

Rita was sitting in the doctor's plush office. She thought that it used to be The Jungle Room but she wasn't sure. She wanted to ask when the doctor came in but, when he did, his expression queered her query.

"What's wrong?" Rita said immediately.

"Sit down," Dr. Lightman said.

"I am sitting," Rita said because she was.

"Of course," Dr. Lightman said. He sat behind his desk, his shoulders slumped, his face grim. He vigorously rubbed his face with his hands.

"Doctor, please," Rita said. "Is Billy ok?"

"Rita—may I call you Rita?" Rita nodded. "Rita, sometimes there are anomalies in the space-time continuum. We don't understand them exactly. We can map time and space to the nearest micrometer reading but there are—*mischiefs*, for want of a better word—in the process that science cannot explain. Like a hiccup in time occurring at exactly the wrong moment."

For fear he would go on this way for a long time, Rita jumped in. "Dr. Lightman, is Billy ok?"

Dr. Lightman looked into Rita's eyes. His puckish face was replaced with an imp's. He looked older suddenly.

"He's gone," he said.

Rita stood up. "Billy's dead?"

"No, Rita. Billy is gone."

"I don't un—" Rita began.

"I'm afraid we lost him in time and space."

"But, you can get him back?"

The doctor's face told her that they could not. "That's it then?"

"I'm so sorry. A full refund, of course, will be paid into your account."

Rita sat. Then she stood again. She looked around the room. Where was she? This was all her fault. She lost Billy Kos in time and space. She lost him for all eternity.

# PART TWO: KEPLER-1647B

Isn't your deepest understanding of time and space and, for that matter, destiny shaped like mine by your earliest experience with geography, by the rules you learned about how to get home again?

—Kurt Vonnegut

A kite is a victim you are sure of.
You love it because it pulls
gentle enough to call you master,
strong enough to call you fool . . .

—Leonard Cohen

Would the twist that had seized our lives never set us down in Kansas again, in good old black and white? Or couldn't you ever go back: Was that only for fairy tales, was the real world everybody got so excitable about precisely this gaudy Technicolor, this relentless, senseless impulsion forward?

—Paul Murray

## DAY 1

I don't know where I am. A disturbing quiet. Not even the buzzing of flies. How I got here is a profound mystery. The last thing I remember was the doctor telling me that I would sleep. I woke face down in the dust, the air around me reddish-yellow and an undulating heat like Nevada. I have nothing except what I am wearing and what is in my pockets: my wallet with money and cards, my keys, an Inspector Gadget rubber squeeze change purse, a mass market copy of Leonard Cohen's *The Spice Box of the Earth* with its browned pages and sweet, sad smell, and a small notebook and pencil. This latter set I was most thankful for and with them I have proposed to make this diary.

I set out walking because what else could I do? There was certainly nothing nearby of interest nor any landmark I recognized so it did not matter in which direction I set out. I thought: If this is Nevada I will soon enough come to a highway or town. The sun seemed both smaller and closer, if that makes any sense. I was hot but the heat was like the hot mist from a tea kettle, yet I was in a desert. In the distance were some vague monticules unless my eyes were playing tricks on me.

I must have walked for two hours—my watch had stopped at the exact moment that the good doctor put me under—and I was growing weary and hungry. There were plants that might have been edible but I did not recognize any of them. There were no cacti. I had read somewhere that you could drink the juice of the cactus plant if you were stuck in the desert. I sat down against a large rock and rested. I was sleepy—possibly from the ether still—and closed my eyes. Something skittered under my legs and I jumped up. It might have been a lizard, perhaps something edible. I dug with my hands. It was like chasing those little burrowing clams one finds at the seashore, but after a few minutes I grabbed a tail and pulled the little bastard into the air.

It was not like any lizard I'd ever seen though my brushes with any kind of wildlife were admittedly few. It was grayish, only slightly darker in color than the sand in which it lived. It had six legs and its hind legs were thicker in the thigh region than the middle or front legs. I imagined this made it very fast on land and I felt lucky to have caught it. It tried to wriggle free and my grip on its tail was tenuous so I put a hand around its abdomen. Its skin was soft as a bunny's though not furry. Instead it seemed to be covered with very fine, very soft cilia. When I closed my hand around it, it whipped its head around and opened its mouth. The small jaws were replete with minute, very sharp teeth, like metallic drill bits, and its eyes were particularly malevolent. I flung the creature as far as I could. It was really just a reflex but I was to learn later that it may have saved my life. The thing hit the sand and was gone in a split second.

I walked further.

Over a small bank of dunes, I did indeed come to a road, a tan macadam surface almost invisible in the surrounding sand. There were no lines on it and no signs beside it. I imagine it was an old road, perhaps a mining road, which was not in use anymore. At any rate, no matter what it was, I felt good about finding it and figured it would eventually lead me to a town. Then, oddly enough, for the first time, I wondered what I would tell people. How had I gotten there? Where was I from and how far had I traveled? No one would believe me.

Nevertheless, I began to follow the road. I headed off to my left for no good reason. What if one way was a thousand miles from a town and the other only two miles? I was going to drive myself crazy thinking like that.

I never did find food today but I did pass a small pond in the middle of nowhere. I tentatively knelt and tentatively put a small handful of water onto my lips. It tasted slightly brackish with an almost citrous tang to it. At the moment, it tasted heavenly and I drank until I felt my stomach fill. After drinking I felt stronger and more optimistic. I walked with a new sense of purpose.

At day's end I assumed I knew which way was west, where a Phlegethontic sunset dazzled me—the day seemed shorter but, again, I had no real sense of time—and I had come no closer to a town, other people, food or good reason to stop or continue. I stopped. I found a small space between rocks where I imagined I might be hidden from predators. That 'lizard' had given me the creeps and I grew afraid of what creatures the night might hold. Nevertheless, after I wrote this entry, I fell asleep readily and my dreams were non-descript, barely remembered. And I did not wake again until the sun was already well up.

## DAY 2

I can almost not write about my second day lost in this—wasteland. I am perhaps feverish, perhaps sick in my soul. Perhaps the Disremembering device has skimble-skambled my brain. I will try to write a rational account of everything that happened—though I am not feeling rational.

I woke with a start. For some moments, I could not recall where I was or how I got there. I seemed to be wedged between two rocks on a bed of fine, russet sand. The ground was almost the same consistency and color as cinnamon. It softly reflected the small, pale sun. I sat up quickly, fearful that something or someone was nearby watching me. It was an eerie feeling to wake with. I've never been paranoid.

I stood slowly. My body ached as if I had been engaged in some intense physical activity the day before. I tried to reconstruct that day, the day that landed me here. I found I could only remember parts of it, as if my personal history had been shot numerous times with a scattergun. There were tiny punctures in my memory.

Something scuttled near me and I jumped. I looked down and at my feet there was an animal I had never seen the like of before. It was shaped like a lizard but had fur like an otter or mink. It seemed a gentler cousin to the carnassial creature I'd seen yesterday. It seemed to be as curious about me as I was about it. I moved away from it a few steps and it closed the distance between us. When I moved a few steps in its direction it backed up.

"Ok," I said. "We're both here. Do you know where here is?"

The thing cocked its head like a dog.

I sighed. I was becoming aware of a ravening hunger and I remembered that I hadn't eaten since before the Disremembering. I looked about for the pool of liquid I had drunk from the day before. If not the same one I found another a few yards away. I went to it and knelt down by its side and lapped up water (if water it was) and then splashed some on my face. When I turned the creature was still with me, a few feet away.

It only occurred to me then that it was my best bet for breakfast. I had no idea how to kill it having never hunted before. The answer seemed simple enough. There were rocks of various sizes around me and I stooped to pick one up that was about the size of a softball. When I weighed it in my hand it was not as heavy as I thought it would be. The creature was not nonplussed by my finding a dornick weapon. I don't think the poor thing had any idea what I had in mind.

Even as I lifted the rock above my shoulder it just cocked its head again and watched me. I brought it down quickly—and accurately—and crushed its small head in one go. It bled a dark brown blood, only slightly darker than the surrounding sand. I felt bad for what I had done but I was famished. And then I realized I would have to eat the little thing raw.

I took its carcass in my hands and, with the sharp edge of another rock, I split its hairy hide open. Its six legs twitched and I almost threw it down but it seemed to only be a muscular reaction to my dividing its skin. There was little animal protein to the thing, and once I'd gutted it, I was left with a few strands of muscular meat. I tore into one strand with my teeth and was rewarded with a warm pith and a flow of chocolate blood. The taste was slightly acrid but not terrible and, after I'd made it through both grisly muscles I drank some more at the pond and cleaned myself up a bit.

Then I was faced with the same dilemma as yesterday. I had to travel down a road leading I didn't know where.

I walked.

I have no idea of the time. The days seemed more—elastic—and the sun moved more swiftly. But it was around the time when the sun was almost directly overhead that I saw the car making its way toward me on the long, straight, dusty road. At first all I saw was a small tan-colored cloud and then, wavering in swells of light, a compact car swaying and choking its way toward me. I thought from the sound of it that it might not make it to me but soon it was within a hundred yards and I could make out the driver, man or woman, leaning toward the windshield as if they could not believe there was a walker on this stretch of highway.

The little car, about the size of an oven, pulled up next to me. The driver's eyes were wide in a comic attitude of marvel. He, or she, slowly got out of the car, leaving the little vehicle sputtering and coughing, and watched me with a wary eye.

"Hi," I said, and took a step forward. The driver made a quick move to re-enter the car. "Wait," I said, standing still. "You have no idea how long I've been out here with no one in sight. I am overjoyed to see you."

Now the driver got back out and stepped around the car. He, or she, was wearing a greige jumpsuit, which seemed to be stretched to its limit by his or her barrel-like body. A most unattractive person, I thought, but no one had ever looked more beautiful to me at that moment. And I thought, secondly, that he or she looked a lot like the androgynous character of Ralph on the TV series *Green Acres*. He or she wore the same kind of bowl haircut, a bit like Ralph, a bit like Moe Howard.

"Who-who are you?" the driver asked.

"Billy. Billy Kos, from Memphis. I've been lost out here for almost 24 hours."

"I don't understand," he or she said.

"Who are you? Where am I?"

"Sir, you're out on the road."

"I know, I know. And I have no idea how I got here. Tell me the nearest town. And your name, kind stranger, please."

He or she fixed me with a doubtful eye.

"Nearest town is Eep," he or she said.

"Sorry, I thought you said Eep."

"Eep. I'm heading there. The wife sent me to Remp for supplies."

A man, I thought. Good.

"I don't know Eep or Remp," I said. "Are we in Nevada?"

"Nevada?" the wary fellow said.

"What desert is this?"

"I don't understand."

"Sorry, tell me your name, please."

"Name is Ek."

"Ek. Fine. I am Billy. Can you give me a ride to Eep? Can I ride with you?"

"Why do you want to go to Eep?"

"I need to find a town, a telephone. I need to know where I am and how I got here."

"You don't know how you got here?"

"I don't, Ek. It's the damnedest thing. Yesterday I was in Memphis and I went to this place of Disremembering and the next thing I knew I was in a desert and lost. I cannot guess what recondite or evil machination dumped me here."

"I don't understand."

Poor Ek, I thought. He's a bit of a simpleton.

"No problem. May I ride with you?"

"Yes, I guess so. If my little car will carry us both."

"Ok, then. Thank you much."

I could barely get my legs under the dashboard of the vehicle, which was the oddest car I'd ever been in. Everything was the same color as Ek's clothing. The whole dashboard was foreign to me and I could only guess that it was a Korean car, or Dutch, or something. Who imports pieces of crap like this?

So, I started out, jerkily, riding with Ek to Eep.

We were both silent for a while, the coughing of the car the only sound in the wide unnerving desert. Then I tried to break the ice. I was hungry for conversation and hoped Ek would pick up his end.

"You know, you ought to have someone look at this car. I think it's probably an easy repair and it will run as good as new."

Ek would only look at me with quick glances. He seemed genuinely afraid.

"I am a mechanic," he finally said.

"Oh, I see. I'm sure then you understand what needs to be done." I was trying affability as a bonding element.

"Just fixed it," Ek said out of the side of his mouth.

"Ah," I answered. I truly did not know how to talk to him.

After an hour or so—there was that tricky time thing eating at the edge of my consciousness—we started seeing other vehicles, all in pretty much the same shape as Ek's—though the road grew no smoother, or wider, or better kept. And then there it was, squatting in the desert like a giant, man-made toad, the town of Eep.

The buildings were all the same dun color and as ill-kept as the car. Indeed, Ek's car seemed to be emblematic of the whole town, of their entire world. But, before I get ahead of myself I will try to tell things as they happened.

To say I was shocked by what I was to find in Eep would be an understatement. Not only did all the buildings look alike—so did the denizens of Eep! If not absolutely alike close enough to convince one that they all came from the same zygote. They all wore the greige outfit, men and women. And they all were alike—*men and women*! I could not tell the difference. Only by listening to their conversations could I determine who was male and who was female. Eventually I learned to discern the subtle shapely difference between genders.

We stopped outside a squat, mud-colored two-story building (two stories were as tall as any building in town) and got out of our jerry-built automobile. Ek parked his next to a row of vehicles, all alike, all the same color, all the same level of craftsmanship, or lack thereof. Some people came out of the building as Ek and I got out of the car.

"Where am I, Ek?" I said now. I stopped and looked around me.

"Eep," he said. "I told you that was where I was going. It is where I live."

"Yes, yes," I said, impatiently. "But what odd manner of dress is this? Where are the women? Is this a town of men alone? I am flummoxed by what I see. I am at sea."

Ek wrinkled his brow. He looked at me askance as if I had insulted his family, which, it turned out, I had.

"This is my wife, Ig," Ek said.

A creature exactly like Ek moved warily forward. "Hello," she said. She was looking at me, I imagine, with the same incredulity I was looking at her. "Where are you from?" she asked. "Remp? I admit I have not been to Remp in years but I thought—well, I don't want to appear rude."

Ek stepped in. "Ig, this is Blee. He is a bit lost."

"I'm sorry," Ig said. She now extended her hand. "You are welcome."

I took her hand, not in a handshake but a gentle clasp. It was a man's hand, or at least it was a hand exactly like Ek's. Ig looked like the *Green Acres* handywoman, too. It was disconcerting.

"I'm sorry," I said. "Where am I? This is not Nevada."

"Eep," Ig said. "This is Eep."

I shook my head. There were more people around. I was garnering a crowd because I must have looked like an alien to them. Which I was.

"Are we still in America?" I ventured. I was beginning to feel queasy.

"America?" Ek said.

"North America?" I tried. "Asia?"

Now the neighbors had gathered too. Only later did I realize that one of the aspects of my appearance which had these good people foxed was that my clothing was of many colors rather than the uniform dull brown that pervaded their entire lives. And, of course, I did not look like Ralph Monroe.

"Asia?" Ig said.

"I'm not making much sense, I guess." I ventured a smile.

"Are you hungry?" Ig asked.

I took a shot. "Am I still on Earth?"

There were murmurings in the crowd. Some folks scooted closer to look at me and some scooted away. Eventually they wandered away, their mild curiosity slaked.

"I don't understand," Ek said.

"The planet. Earth."

"Earth." Ek rolled the name around in his mouth a bit. "This is not Earth."

"Mars. I know there was talk of Mars back home."

"This is neither Earth nor Mars," Ig said. "Are you hungry?"

"What planet is this?" I feared the answer. I feared not knowing more.

"This is Kepler-1647b."

Something inside of me fell a long way. "I—I have never heard of Kepler—what you said."

"We have never heard of Earth. We did not know anyone was advanced enough to travel in space."

"I—I didn't either," I said. "Wait. How is it that you speak English?"

They hesitated and Ig and Ek met each other's gaze. "I don't understand," they said in unison.

Inside their house, I was introduced to their two children. They were also called Ek and Ig and were miniature versions of their parents. The youngest, Ig, did not want to sit at the table with us and took her place on a dirty looking couch in the next room where she could see and hear everything but not be contaminated by the alien.

The food was all one color and all one flavor. It was the worst meal I have ever eaten and that includes the lunch I had at a vegan restaurant back in Memphis. There was not much conversation at first. I thought everyone must be chewing over what we had discussed outside. Somehow, some way, I had been transported in space by that crap Disremembering machine. I was fearful and I was awestricken.

"Thank you for your generosity," I told Ek and Ig.

"You are most welcome," they answered.

"As you can imagine I am still in shock. I can't conceive what has happened."

"It is interesting," Ek said. But his tone said, this is not interesting at all. It was as if they had already digested this peculiar news and accepted that I was among them for howsoever long I would be.

I managed to get the food down—it was something like pabulum made of clay—and after the meal I was startled when Ig, the smaller Ig, appeared suddenly beside me. She held out her hand and in her palm was a small round brown object.

"Is this for me, Ig?" I asked. I didn't really know how to talk to children, even back home, much less on this new planet.

"Yes," she said. Her voice was fainter than, but just as inflectionless as, her parents'.

"What is it?" I said as the thing tumbled onto my palm.

"Dirt clod," Little Ig said.

After the meal Ek suggested that he drive me around Eep and introduce me to some folks. He said he could show me the garage where he worked and find out if anyone was hiring.

"You're very kind, Ek. I fear I am a burden on you. A job? Well, surely I won't be here that long, do you think?"

"I do not know, Blee. How far away is Earth?"

"I have no idea."

"Do you know how to go back?"

"No, heavens no. I might be stuck here."

"Hence a job," Ek said. His logical tone, even while being kind, was beginning to aggravate me. But I was a guest and grateful and lost, so lost.

We got back into his spavined car and it coughed like a cat with a fishbone in its throat and spat out a few dark blue clouds and we rolled down the poorly maintained streets of Eep. Citizens on the uneven sidewalks stared and waved. It appeared that news of my residency had spread already. They were all dressed alike. They all looked alike. I know I am repeating myself but it was the most unnerving aspect, so far, of this perplexing planet, this daymare I found myself within.

The garage, a one-story building made of the same greige colored material as every building in Eep, was dark and grimy and olid; it smelled like a cross between oil and human body odor. There were a half dozen cars, exactly like Ek's, in various stages of disassembling or reassembling. Wires and pipes hung from some like the guts of eviscerated animals. The air was thick and a fine black mist hung over the work area.

Ek introduced me to a number of his co-workers. None of them had much to say. I was introduced to the boss whose name is Of. No one mentioned surnames and I gathered that they either had none or declined to use them.

"Have no job," Of said, holding my hand. No one had mentioned a job yet.

"That's fine," I said. "I don't know how long I'll be here."

"No job," he repeated, smiling.

"Do you know of a job in town?" Ek said.

Of looked at his employee and then at me and scratched his forehead with the tool he held in his hand. "Maybe in Remp," he offered.

I think Of was afraid of me, the new alien. Perhaps he feared competition or some new ideas he was unready to assimilate into his routine life. I began to think that everyone in this town was in a bland routine which they held to fiercely as if to rock the boat meant certain drowning. I imagine I represented some serious boat-rocking.

Ek got permission to take the afternoon off and squire me around town. I was introduced to many people, none memorable, all the same. I even met the mayor—Ub—who was kind and seemed to accept that an alien in their midst was just part of life, something like pregnancy or death, something that did not deserve too much anxiety. Ub told me he'd inquire about work and asked me to return the next day.

"That's something I should have addressed earlier," Ek said as we drove back along the town's main street. "Would you accept our hospitality for the night? I can only offer you a couch, I'm afraid."

"Thank you, Ek. I don't know what else I can do. I have no money, if you use money, and I don't really know what tomorrow will bring."

"Tonight will bring you dinner and a couch and some family time. You are most welcome. I think for a treat we will pick up dinner on our way home and surprise Ig."

We stopped at a small, brown café called Ad's. I thought perhaps I would be treated to a different cuisine, something more palatable than what Ig had fixed for lunch. We picked up a casserole of sorts. It was made of the same dull clay and I could only choke it down by drinking a lot of water with it, though the water had that same odd tang I first encountered drinking from the pool in the desert.

Before we turned in for the night I played a board game on the floor with the children. The rules were arcane and quite beyond me but little Ek and Ig laughed at how flustered I was and announced that, after about an hour, they had beaten me by a couple thousand sockets. I rubbed their little tan heads and wished them pleasant dreams.

"I don't understand," little Ek said. "What is dreams?"

"Things you see in your sleep," I offered.

They looked at each other, broke into a fit of giggles, and skedaddled off to bed.

I bedded down on the sprung couch with a scratchy blanket that seemed to be made from a cross between burlap and newspaper. Ek turned the light out and wished me good sleep. I turned it back on once he had gone and made these notes in my notebook. Right as I was dropping off, exhausted but full of wild thoughts, Ek turned the light back on and squatted next to my head.

"Blee," he said. "I'm sorry for waking you. I should have thought of this sooner. Tomorrow we will visit our local science teacher. If anyone can give you answers she can."

"That's a wonderful idea, Ek. Thank you," I said.

"Yes," Ek said and then patted my shoulder. "Tomorrow we will visit Ae."

## DAY 3

Surprisingly, I slept well. The couch felt like a sack of meal and there was a constant creaking as if the walls were not joined securely; nevertheless, I fell back into slumber after Ek woke me and I dreamed I was on the ocean, just me, a small raft and a woman. I do not remember who the woman was or if she was someone I really know but in the dream, we were in love. Our love was strong though our situation was perilous. Right before I woke up I was leaning over to kiss her and a tentacle sprang from the water and wrapped itself around her waist. Did it pull her in? Did I lose my love to the briny deeps? I'll never know because I woke to find Little Ig sitting on my stomach playing a small instrument that looked like a cross between a kazoo and a tonette.

"Alien man," Little Ig said, pausing her grating tune. "Alien man is awake."

"Good morning, Blee," Big Ig said, suddenly beside me.

Big Ig was wearing a see-through gown, presumably pajamas. I was comforted by the fact that her anatomy was exactly like women on Earth. She had breasts and even pubic hair. But I was disconcerted by how unattractive she was. She looked like her husband with breasts and a poontang.

And it was then her husband called out: "Wake up, Blee! Making breakfast and then we'll go see Ae. Good day ahead. I have to be at the garage soon but I can drop you off at the school."

This was way too much activity and conversation in my first moments of waking in this strange new world. The only voice missing was little Ek. I did not have to wait long for him to pipe up.

"Dad, Oj says the alien could be a virus. He could make us all sick," Little Ek said, entering the room, looking back and forth between me and his father.

"He is our guest," Big Ek said. "He is not a virus."

And that seemed to settle it. Little Ek was mollified and moved on. This was apparently the way with denizens of Kepler-1647b. They were quickly and easily satisfied.

After a nauseating breakfast (coffee, my God, these heathens had not discovered coffee!) and a quick shower under the acidic water I was once again a passenger in Ek's little car, on my way to find help. I was the lost man. The space wanderer. People would help me, I felt sure. The conversation on the way to the school was stilted and a little frustrating.

"So, Ek, I appreciate more than I can say, the hospitality you've shown me, a stranger, a stranger from another world even."

"You are a guest," Ek replied in his simple, logical way.

"Yes, well, thank you. I am curious about your planet. Are there countries?"

"I believe so," Ek said. "Many countries."

"Is there any war, any animosity between countries?"

"I don't understand."

"No military, tanks, guns, bombs?"

"Guns, we have many guns."

"Who has them, Ek?"

"Gun people. There are people who like guns."

"Do you own a gun?"

Ek gave a quick snort through his nose as if I had made a joke. "I don't."

"What is the name of your country, the country where we are, where Eep is?

"Our country is called North."

"North."

"That's right. Eep is part of North."

"And other countries are south of you? Is there a country called South?"

"I believe so."

"But you are not sure."

"I have never seen it but it is in some papers."

"Papers. What kind of papers?"

"The papers about Kepler-1647b."

"Where are these papers?"

"There are probably some at the school."

"Good, good. I will want to look at them."

Ek was not curious why I would want to look at the papers. He seemed to be not curious about anything.

"What about Remp? You've been in Remp. Is it different from Eep?"

"Oh, very different."

"Then I would like to visit there."

"Of course. Here is the school."

We pulled up in front of a two-story building which looked exactly like the apartment building where Ek lived.

"Ae is inside. She is very pretty and young but she knows much."

"Thank you, Ek," I said. I put my hand out. Ek took my hand and held it.

I left him and went inside. I waved as he drove off but he never turned his head.

Inside there was a long hall and many rooms. It was not unlike an elementary school on Earth. I walked down the hall and all the rooms were empty. Was this a holiday? Finally, in the next to last room there was someone standing in front of a row of seats. All the seats were empty except for a small child in the front row. I knocked lightly on the wall outside the opening. There were no doors to the classrooms.

"Hello," the teacher said.

"Hi, I am looking for Ae."

"Yes, hello. I am Ae, Blee."

"You know my name."

"It's a small town. You've come from far away they tell me."

"Yes, ma'am. Earth. In the Milky Way."

"Ah."

"I hate to interrupt the class. I can come back."

"Nonsense. We're not learning anything today. Ak is my best student. She knows much. She is, well for now, my only student."

"Are the kids not required to go to school?"

"Oh no. We feel it puts too much pressure on them. They come when they are curious about something. Like you."

"Well, thank you. Thank you, Ak."

Ak looked at me without interest. She stood up and walked out of the room.

"So, we are alone now," Ae said. "What can I tell you?"

"Well, I don't know. I am lost. I am apparently stuck on your planet. I will try to tell you as best as I can how I got here but I don't understand even a fraction of it."

"Fine. Shall we go into my office where it is more comfortable?"

We went into an adjoining room which was darker and had some soft chairs and a couch.

"Sit here," Ae said, motioning toward the couch. I sat and, instead of taking one of the chairs nearby the way I expected her to, she sat very close to me on the couch. She crossed one clad leg over another. I don't need to mention that her outfit looked exactly like everyone else's and she, poor thing, looked almost exactly like everyone else. She could have been male except I was told she was a woman. If there was a womanly shape underneath that dull shift I could not discern it. I assumed there was from my glimpse of Ig's sexual features this morning.

"Is this comfortable?" she asked.

"Yes," I said.

I told her, as best I could, everything that happened to me after I tried to erase the memory of my wife. That was another thing. Not only did that damn machine set me loose in time and space it did not erase my memories of Kalma and those memories retained their sting. My forgettery was flawed.

"Hm," Ae said. "That is quite a tale."

"Can you help me? Do you understand the science behind what happened?"

"I understand some of it."

"Some."

"Yes. Tell me this. Are you over your wife?"

This seemed an odd question. "It's not quite the thing I'm worried most about."

"Right." Ae wrinkled her brow. "So, you are single, unattached?"

"I—I am not sure. I don't know what time it is on Earth or whether I will ever see Kalma again so that's as good as a divorce, wouldn't you say?"

"I would." Ai smiled. She sat, staring at me, smiling.

"Can you help me? Is there a way to reverse what has happened?"

"Oh, I have no idea," Ae said. She continued to smile.

"Ah, that's disappointing. Do you know if there is anyone who would know?"

"Not in Eep."

"You are the expert on science in Eep?"

"Yes, I guess that is what I am. Sorry."

"Ek thought you could help me."

Ae smiled. "Ek is trying to find me a husband. Everyone in Eep is trying to find me a husband."

"What?"

"I am the only female of marrying age left unmarried in Eep. And there are no marriageable males. So, though outwardly I find you somewhat unattractive, I believe I see the possibility of an arranged marriage in which we could both be happy."

And she placed one large, mannish hand on my knee.

"Ae, I'm sorry. I was unware of what Ek had in mind. For now, though you are a very attractive woman, I must spend my time trying to find out if I can return to my home."

"There's no rush. I will be fertile for another 160 cycles."

"Good to know," I said and I rose. "Is that a year?"

"Is what a year?"

"A cycle?"

"I don't understand."

When I left the school, I started walking back toward the town square. I felt as alone as I've ever felt in my life and I gave into despair. Not only was I far from home and the comforts of familiarity but I was among the dullest beings in the universe, each just like the other, no one with any conventional ability to hold a conversation. Of course, I understood that our conventions were not theirs but, surely, communication is paramount for any civilization. Perhaps it is only in Eep that this dullness infects the entire populace. Ek said that Remp was very different so I latched onto the idea that I would travel to Remp as soon as possible. I wondered if it were possible to rent a car and drive myself.

I headed toward the garage and found the workers there all sitting outside and having lunch. No one spoke.

"Hello," I said.

"Blee, how was the meeting with Ae? Did she get you sorted out?"

"Ek, you had a different agenda in mind," I told him in a kind voice. I was not judging him.

"Ah, Ae mentioned our shortage of potent men."

She had not said 'potent.' "She did. She also allowed as to how she had no idea how I could get back home."

"That is a shame," Ek said. He continued to eat. His coworkers did not even acknowledge the conversation happening around them. They ate quietly.

"Ek, do you think I could rent a car to take a trip to Remp?"

"Blee, of course. You could borrow ours but I need it to get to work."

"How far is Remp?"

"Oh, you would have to spend one night there. I would not leave now. If you wake early tomorrow and drive all day you will get there before dinner and be able to meet some of our neighbors and find yourself a place to sleep."

"That's fine," I told Ek. "And the car?"

"I will have my boss round one up."

"I have no money."

"He will accept my word that you will pay later."

"Wonderful. Thank you, Ek."

"You are my guest," Ek said.

That evening I ate with the family again—I was able to eat a little more of the nondescript food as if my system was adjusting itself to the muck—and afterward I sat on the couch alternately reading from Leonard Cohen's poems and writing in my notebook.

"What is that?" Little Ig said, scrunching next to me on the couch.

"A book of poems," I said. "Famous Canadian poet and singer." I showed her the cover.

"I don't understand," she said.

"Do you know what a poem is, Ig?"

She made a pucker of her lips. "A poem. I am not sure."

"I'll read you one," I said. And I read her the first poem in the book, "A Kite is a Victim."

By the time I finished the short poem the family had gathered around. I looked up from the book and smiled at my impromptu audience.

"What is that, Blee," Big Ig said. "It is like music."

"Poetry," I said.

They looked at each other. It was a humorous mummer's show.

"I don't understand," they all said at once.

That night I turned out my light early. I had much to think about.

Ek once again turned the light back on and squatted next to the couch.

"Blee," he whispered. "Are you mad at Ek for trying to find a match for the science teacher."

"No, Ek," I said. "I understand." Though I didn't and was tempted to say so.

"She is a very good woman, Ae."

"I'm sure she is."

"And you are a good man, Blee."

"Thank you, Ek."

"She's very pretty, the science teacher. Isn't she?"

"Yes, very," I said.

"Perhaps you would like to have sex with her."

I was confounded by such a blunt statement. Perhaps here sex is not a big deal. I tried to think like a sociologist, an anthropologist. Perhaps, as with Kalma, sex is recreational.

"I don't know her well," I answered after a moment.

"You have sex with her and then you will know her."

"Ok," I said, inanely. "But tomorrow I must go to Remp."

"Yes," Ek said. "That is tomorrow."

## DAY 4

We woke at the crack of dawn, though I am not sure dawn cracks here the way it does at home. I was awakened by Little Ig sitting on my chest. When I opened my eyes she said, "Dad says you gotta get on the road."

"Thanks, Ig," I said and she hopped down.

We filled up with more beige food. I offered to help with the dishes. They hand washed everything because they had no dishwasher. The appliances they did have were old and/or poorly constructed. The only thing in the house that worked well was the toilet that flushed with air instead of water.

After breakfast Ek said he thought perhaps it was time for me to change clothes. I was about to pick up and don the only set of clothes I had, though they were dusty and stained. Ek brought me a greige jumpsuit. I thanked him and put it on. It hung loose on me since I did not have the girth other Keplerites had. They were all fairly orbicular.

"You look very nice," Big Ig said.

"Thank you, Ig."

"All the girls will be after you," she sniggered.

"Now Ig," I said. "You know I only have eyes for you."

I was never good with jokes even on Earth but this one fell flat so hard I heard it hit the ground. Ig looked at her shoes and Ek's brow wrinkled in a way that made me feel ashamed.

"I'm sorry," I said. "A joke. The kind of joke we make on Earth."

I looked hopefully around at their faces. They may have been slightly appeased—it was hard to tell—and Ig whispered, "I see."

It took a while to get the car started but once I did I felt good about being on my own for a while. It was difficult making myself understood among the Keplerites and, to be honest, I was heavy bored. The drive did little to ease my boredom. Their cars had no radios. One long straight dirt road with a sign about halfway there saying, "Remp 115 Secs." I had no idea what this meant but assumed it was not seconds. Sections?

I passed two cars during the drive. Neither driver even looked up at me. I was less an attraction in my jumpsuit and crap car. The small sun passed its midpoint but I did not reach for the bag of taupe food that Big Ig had prepared for my lunch. She had also given me some small oyster-colored coins.

I finally spotted Remp up ahead. Its skyline was not promising. Again, there was no tint, no differentiation. And once I pulled into the town proper I was chagrinned to find that the buildings all looked the same. The cars, the people, the roads, the stores, etc., etc., etc., all looked the same. I slowed the car and my shoulders slumped. I stopped in front of a store and parked the car.

I drew a few glances as I entered the store, probably due to my thin body and full head of unkempt hair. The store sold food, drugs, small appliances, medical supplies and pictures of a man who wore the same jumpsuit as everyone else but sported a hat with a white sun shape on its brim. I learned later that it was the president. Of what I was not sure.

There was a small cooler with drinks and I picked up a bottle of what I thought was Yahoo or chocolate milk. I took it to the counter and offered my handful of coins. The young gink behind the counter said, "That's too much."

"I know. How much is the drink?"

"Less than that."

"Can you just pick out what you need?"

"Why would you want to pay too much?" He was not belligerent. He was, I would say, puzzled.

"I'm new here and I don't know your currency yet."

He thought about that for a while. "This much," he said, plucking a small, thin coin from my hand.

"Thank you," I told him and smiled. "Is the mayor hard to see?"

"You mean is he invisible?"

"No, no, I said. Can I visit him without calling ahead?"

"Sure, I guess so. I have never been to see him."

"Ok, thanks. Where is his office?"

"Next door."

"Right. Thanks for your time."

I stepped outside and to the left was an office building and to the right was an office building. There were a number of signs on the one to the right. They made no sense to me so I tried the building on the left. I entered a hallway much like the one at the school in Eep. The first door on the right said, "Ud, Mayor."

I knocked and received no answer. I knocked a little harder. The door was opened by a man who—yes, looked exactly like every other grown man on Kepler 1647b.

"Yes?"

"I'm looking for the mayor."

"Who are you?"

"My name is Billy. I've driven here from Eep."

"I'm the mayor," the man said with either humility or boredom.

"I'm sorry, I expected a secretary. May I talk to you?"

"Yes."

"May I come in?"

"Of course, yes. Come in and sit down."

His office was unsurprising. There was a picture of the president behind his desk.

"What can I do for you, Blee."

"Billy."

The two syllables were throwing him.

"What can I do for you?"

I told him a brief version of my story up until the part where I rented a car and drove to Remp. His expression never changed but I didn't think he believed me.

"I don't believe you," he said. "I'm busy, so—"

I couldn't imagine what he was busy with. His office was clean and his desk bare. It did not seem like a place where any manner of work was ever done.

"Ok," I said. "I'm sorry I bothered you."

"Wait," he said. "Don't go away mad. I suggest you might go talk to our scientist."

"Yes, ok, thank you."

"She lives in Eep and her name is—"

"Ae."

"Ae," he finished.

"Thank you. I'll try that," I said and left.

I looked around Remp. The sun was setting and the shadows made the small town look like something from a television western. Long shadows stretched into the dusty street. There were few people about. I looked for an inn.

I found one on the next block. It said, "Inn." On the door it said, "Inn In."

After some more awkward conversation I was able to book a room. It was small and nondescript, of course. I went downstairs for dinner because I saw a sign advertising their "Good food."

The waiter was polite and the menu meant nothing to me. I asked him to recommend something and he pointed to something on the menu. I said that that would be fine.

When he brought the food, it looked exactly like the meals I had eaten at Ig and Ek's.

"Say," I said, just to make conversation, to stretch out the experience so that I did not have to return to my room, "Who is the man in that picture?" I pointed to the wall.

The waiter looked at me. "Sir?" he said as if I had asked him about politics or money or sex.

"The president," he answered finally.

"Ah," I said. "Does he live in Remp?"

"Sir, I fear you are ridiculing me."

"I assure you I am not. I'm not from around here."

"I gathered as much from your hair. But everyone knows the president lives in Remp."

I opened my eyes wide. "Oh!" I said.

"Will that be all sir? How is your food?"

"Do you think I could get in to see the president?"

Another pause. "Of course, sir. Anyone can see the president."

"Very good, thanks. And the food is excellent."

"Thank you, sir."

Before I turned in for the night I asked the receptionist at the inn how to get to the president's office."

"Do you know where the mayor's office is?"

"Yes," I said.

"It's the other office building."

That night in my nondescript room I sat on the bed deep in thought. There was no television, of course, no reading material except a menu for the restaurant. On the menu were four items, all of which sounded alike. I still could not figure out with what they made their food. I had neglected to bring my Leonard Cohen so I lay on the rigid brown bed and let my mind play with the revelations of the day. I had hope, that thing with feathers. I believed in a future again.

I ended the night with optimism and wrote this blithe summation of my day. I have vowed to keep this record though, if it ever makes it back to Earth, I fear people will think I fantasticate."

## DAY 5

It was as easy to see the president as it had been to see the mayor. Perhaps they don't revere their politicians. Perhaps their politicians have little power.

I was hoping the president would have clout unavailable to other citizens. I was hoping this man, the sovereign of his nation, would have the intelligence, imagination and power that I had found lacking in the other denizens of my new world.

The president's name is Vrt. I guessed that his office afforded him an extra letter in his name, an extra letter but no vowel. Perhaps, I thought, Vrt means president.

"Your visit has been foretold," Vrt greeted me at the door. My heart leapt. This man has arcane faculties, occult talents, magick at his fingertips.

"I am so pleased," I bubbled. "You can help me then. I pray your powers extend toward the unexplained."

"I don't understand," he said.

My heart did one painful thump. "I thought that you had ESP that told you I was coming to see you today. I was hoping you have other powers as well."

"ESP is a strange word," Vrt said. "Does it mean that town gossip travels quickly?"

Oh, I said, interiorly. Oh, my heart pumped a poor pump. Oh, my spine shivered. Oh, oh, oh.

"I'm sorry. Let me tell you my story."

And, once again, I laid out my bizarre tale of travel across space and time. I embellished a bit, I stretched it a bit. The story was accruing barnacles of extraneous detail.

"Huh," Vrt said. "Your people can travel across space and time."

"I—I suppose so. I mean, it's how I got here. I am not sure whether I was the first."

"Huh," he repeated.

"I surmise from your expression and attitude that you have no idea how to get me back or whom I can ask for assistance."

Then he told me about Ae.

"Tell me this," I said. "Are you part of one nation and, if so, are there other nations? Other places on your world where I might travel to in my quest for answers, in search of the solution to my problem?"

"I don't know," he said. "I imagine so. Do you still have your spaceship?"

I smiled. "Thank you," I said, rising. "I appreciate your time."

"And space," he said.

It was the first joke I'd heard on Kepler. I did not do well with jokes on Earth. I never knew what was funny and what was heart-breaking.

"Thank you," I said, again. And I left his office.

I found my car and began the drive back to Eep. It was a desultory drive and by the time I reached Ek and Ig's I was as sad as a soul estranged. Over dinner that night I gave a half-hearted rendition of my day and a half in Remp.

Ek's kind face told me that at least compassion existed on Kepler.

"You are welcome to stay here as long as need be," he said. "And tomorrow I can ask Of if he can take you on at the garage."

"Thank you, Ek," I said. I went to bed tonight, wrote down this desolate account and then lay awake until Little Ig came to me in the morning with another dirt clod for my collection.

## DAY 8

A few days have passed. I did not record them. I started working at the garage and learned the ins and outs of their primitive vehicles. I also learned their currency and was paid daily at the end of each shift. This allowed me to start paying for my couch and board.

Tonight, I read a little more Leonard Cohen to the family. They seemed genuinely interested but, as soon as I was through, they went away and I assumed that even poetry, even sublime Leonard Cohen, did not touch their bland lives.

Before I closed my notebook, Big Ig returned to the living room. She was wearing that sheer gown again and I found myself averting my eyes.

"This poetry," she said. "I think it is interesting."

"I'm glad, Ig."

"And it's all in that little book."

"Yes."

"That is nothing like the books I have seen."

"What books have you seen, Ig?"

"The one Ek has about how to fix cars. And the few that Ae has which are about things I don't need to know about."

"I see. Are you curious about those things in other books? Poetry? Science?"

"No," she said, plainly.

"Ok," I said.

She placed a hand on my cheek. I tried not to look at her shapeless breasts.

"Thank you for being our friend," she said.

"Thank you, Ig," I said.

## DAY 15

I bought some new jumpsuits today (they call them shefs). Now I have 3 identical shefs. I learned how to wash and dry them. I have neglected my diary. I have nothing new to report. I work. I eat. I talk to Ek and the other mechanics about cars and food. I go back to Ek and Ig's and eat and sleep.

## DAY 20

Today I found out that I have enough money to get my own place. Tomorrow I will find an apartment near the garage.

## DAY 22

I moved into my own place today. It is small, smaller than Ek and Ig's. They helped me get it set up (it took about 20 minutes) and showed me how all the appliances and household items worked. I have one mattress, one old chair, and a small table something like a card table but on three legs.

It has one of their ingenious toilets, which works like a complex rhyme.

On the way home from work I bought some paper. I have vowed to start writing poetry again. I can't tonight because I am too tired. Tomorrow night for sure.

## DAY 23

I rushed through my dinner tonight because I was anxious to start writing. Just as I was beginning my first poem in I don't know how long (I had an idea based on a weak sun, a smaller sun—I thought the title 'A Weak Sun' had possibilities) there was a knock on my door. When I opened the door, there stood Ae with a bottle in her hand.

"A gift," she said. She handed me the tan bottle. I shook it like a fool. I was somewhat taken aback by her presence.

"What is it?"

"Am I disturbing you? May I come in?"

"I'm sorry, of course. Come in. I don't have much." I spread my arm and waved it in a ridiculous semi-circle around the room. It was a poor show.

"It's bik," Ae said.

"Bik?"

"The bottle. Bik. A drink. I think you'll like it."

We settled on the couch.

"Is it alcoholic?"

"I don't understand. Alcohol. Like hydroxol?"

"I don't know," I said. "Does it make one drunk?"

"Drunk, after we drink."

"What?"

"The past tense."

"Yes, right. After."

"I don't understand."

"Never mind," I said. "Let's have some."

I had no glasses.

"I have no glasses," I said.

"I don't mind drinking from the bottle if you don't."

"Not at all." I handed the bottle to her. She peeled the top back and a rich, sweet, peppery aroma filled the room. Its perfume was intoxicating if its contents were not. "It smells divine."

"Divine," she said. She tilted it back and her eyes—which I now noticed were a pale blue—widened and her cheeks flushed. "Oof," she said, handing me the bottle.

I drank. It burned like sterno. I spit out a bit.

"Jesus," I said.

"You hate it," she said. Her cheeks were positively glowing.

"Let me try again." I poured more slowly. It still burned but I kept it down. The bump inside my head was like an electric shock.

"Ouch," I said.

"It's good, right?"

"Yes, it—it has a kick. What is in it?"

"I am not allowed to tell."

I laughed. "Who says you cannot?"

"Bik is illegal," she said.

"Oh, my goodness."

"Because it opens up your inner self in ways that some find dangerous."

"I see. Are you in danger bringing it to me?"

"You won't tell," she said, and she smiled.

"No, of course not." It occurred to me then for the first time that I had seen no police force, no evidence of a government mustering of troops.

"Now, do you want me to take my shef off? I am told I have a very beautiful body."

My brain stopped working. The bik made my tongue soggy.

"Ae, I am sure you do."

"Good then," she said. She began unzipping the shef. Its one long zipper ran from neck to crotch. She had it down before I could formulate another word. Her round body was clad in a tan-colored piece of lingerie similar to what back home, I believe, is called a teddy. Her shef was on the floor and she kicked off her boots.

"Should I be completely naked before you take your shef off? Is that how you did it back on Earth?"

"Either way," I said. My brain was sparking and something was making colors inside my bloodstream.

"I'll go ahead," she said.

She lifted the lingerie off over her shoulders and lowered it, and there she was, naked as a stone.

"I have a lovely body, right?" she said.

"You do. You honestly do," I said.

She was shapeless. And there was a fine hair like cilia over much of her midsection and limbs. Between her legs the cilia were thick like pubic hair, like a darkened oasis in the dun-colored desert. I could not imagine what lay behind that chestnut patch. I did not have to imagine it long.

"Do you have a pretty body, Blee?"

"I'm not sure. I am not sure."

"No one has told you so?"

And then I felt my braggadocio rising. "I am told my penis is quite large."

"Is that a good thing on Earth?"

"Is it not here?"

"I don't know. I believe all men's equipment is the same size."

"Of course," I said. Despite the absurdity of my situation I was getting turned on. It was the first sex talk I had heard in a long time.

"Strip, Blee," she said.

I stood. I unzipped my shef. I had only a pair of Earth briefs underneath. Fruit-of-the Loom.

"It's white," she said.

I turned and pulled my briefs down. She hummed behind me. The hum sounded too much like Kalma and I spun around. I was at half-mast.

Ae goggled her eyes. Was she kidding?

"Blee," she said. Her tongue licked her crusty lips. "I think on Earth things are quite different."

"Different?" I said. I sat down.

"Different," she said again.

"Do I not please you?"

"Blee, I must tell you this. You have an enormous penis."

"Oh." I might have blushed.

"I don't think it will fit inside me."

"Shall we try anyway?" I said because, by now, I was quite aroused.

"Yes, let's."

I leaned forward and we kissed. It was a nice kiss, a bit dry, a bit too much pressure. My hand instinctively went to her breast and she began to stick her tongue in and out of my mouth, rapidly, as if pumping my mouth with her tongue.

I ran a hand down her hairy stomach and into her thick pubic bush. It was hot there. Really hot. And more uliginous than a bog. I put a finger inside her.

"Ah, ah, ah, Blee! What are you doing?"

I pulled my finger out.

"Please—please put it back. Please!"

I did and she began to grind against it and was panting like a wild animal. She had an orgasm.

"Blee, is that how you do it on Earth?" Her eyes were wide.

"That is only foreplay," I explained.

"For play, yes. I can see that. Let's have sex. Am I supposed to touch your sex thing for play?"

I shrugged. She reached her hand outward and stopped. She stared at my cock which was shivering and growing in anticipation. She grabbed my penis and began gently pulling on it. She was approximating a pretty good hand job if unpracticed in the ways of foreplay. I was panting myself.

"It's so nice, for play," she said.

"Suck me," I said.

"I'm sorry."

"Oh, never mind. Fuck me, Ae. Get on top of me."

She didn't have to be told twice. Her pussy burned as I slid in but she took the full length of me quite well. She was screaming and bouncing up and down on me. Her breasts were flying around.

"You are HUGE!" she screamed and came.

And right after that so did I. I let it go. It was weeks' worth. I came for a long time. As I pumped and pumped Ae's eyes were wide, staring into my face. I could not imagine how comic my orgasmic face would be but she seemed mesmerized.

In the afterglow she said, "I want to do that more. What did you call it? Fuck? I want to fuck. You have the biggest penis on Kepler, by far. Bigger is nicer. And you squirted for such a long time. Men here only come one quick blast. We have much to teach each other."

She was garrulous with lust.

"What is suck?"

"Oral sex. I'll show you next time."

"Can next time be now?" she asked.

My mind swam, a kaleidoscope of erotica and past failures.

"Yes, Ae," I said. "It can be."

## DAY 24

Today was the happiest day I have had in a while.

I woke with Ae lying naked beside me. The weak sunlight was peering around the dirty window shade and lighting up the cilia on Ae's midsection like tiny wicks of phosphorous. It was still disconcerting to look at her face and see there the face of Ek, or Little Ek, or Of, or any other denizen of this strange planet, male or female. But her breasts, which I characterized as shapeless, were actually pleasantly saggy and their nipples, small boats in a sea of soft flesh, were standing straight up. Best of all her pubic hair was so dense it was like a cave entrance and I knew from three straight periods of lovemaking that this cave was as hot as a volcano. I could not help putting my hand there, to once again tangle those briers around my fingers. I trailed my index finger down her stomach and into that jungle and found it already wet and inviting. Perhaps it was always wet.

"Grrrrrr," Ae said, awakening. "OH!"

"Good morning, Darling," I said, and eased a finger inside her.

"G-g-g—D-don't stop," Ae said, tensing her body. "D-d-d-. . ." she continued until her orgasm was complete.

"Good morning," I said again.

"What a way to wake, my love," she said. I looked into her pale blue eyes. They were almost feminine.

"I cannot keep my hands off you," I told her.

"Don't then. Make me come with your tongue again like you did last night. That was—magic."

"Oral sex is not magic," I said, my finger finding her little clit.

"Uh uh uh," she said. "It is m-magic. I have never seen the like of it."

"I am yours to command," I said. And I threw the sheet off and positioned myself between her legs and licked her into four consecutive orgasms. She lay back spent. I put my head on her stomach and her fleece tickled my cheek.

"I want to do the other thing," she said, sleepily.

"What's that, my love?"

"The other oral sex."

"Ah. That would be lovely."

"Are you erect?"

"I am."

"Give me another moment."

She took a few deep breaths. And sat up. "Lie on your back, Mr. Big Earth Dick," she said. She tilted her face like a puppy. "I like your word 'dick'."

When she took my shaft in her hand she began to pump it in a much more practiced rhythm. She had learned the handjob quickly.

"I cannot get over the size of you," she said.

"Mm," I replied.

"Did I do it alright last night? The other oral sex?"

"It's called a blowjob. Yes, you did fine once you remembered to keep your teeth off me."

"I am sorry, my love. Watch how good I do it this time. I am going to take it all the way into my mouth though it is a bit frightening."

And she did. And she played with my balls, like I showed her. I felt the surge growing. Last night I did not come in her mouth but pulled her off and entered her one more time. This morning I did not. I shot off down her throat. She held her head still and let it all slide down. She was very still. I was spent.

"That's not poison, is it?" she said, taking me gingerly out of her mouth and holding the limp weapon gently in her palm.

"Would I poison you, Darling?"

"No, of course not. It tastes funny. I can almost name it."

"Better than the food on Kepler," I joked.

She thought about that. "Yes," she said. "I believe you're right. I believe it will be my new diet."

We stayed in bed the entire day, neither of us going to work. At night, we ate some bland food and then each other and we made love three more times before I picked up this notebook to write about my day.

"What are you doing?" she asked.

"A diary."

"A diary?"

"The story of my life on Kepler. I am writing because it helps me to make sense of things."

"Huh."

"Would you like to read it?"

"Maybe later," she said. She lay back on the single pillow. "Writing about yourself," she said, dreamily.

"Have you never written?" I asked. "And you a teacher."

"I've not," she said.

"Huh," I replied.

## DAY 25

This morning I woke again to the bliss of Ae's body next to mine. We made love once more before we each parted for our places of business.

"Will you come back tonight?" I asked, kissing her at the door.

"Of course," she said. "May I bring a few things?"

"What kinds of things?" I asked, still holding her.

"Clothes, tooth cleaner, woman things."

"Oh, Ae," I said, and kissed her once more.

At work, there were no questions asked about my absence the day before. Neither was there any curiosity about where I had been.

"Hello, Blee," Ek said. "I think you have a car waiting. Valve trouble if I had to guess."

"Thank you, Ek."

And while I worked on the car I began to reflect on this lack of curiosity which appeared endemic to Keplerites. Only Ae seemed to possess a spark of inquisitiveness and admiration for anything new, and then only in our sex life. She seemed for a moment to be interested in my journal but then the thought left her mind like a wafting breeze. I vowed to explore this and went home this evening, I admit here, with an agenda. I wanted to break through her apathy, and, in a sense, I wanted to use her as a test case. I wanted them all to be more questioning. Even my appearance on their world, from across the great wash of time and space, gave them only momentary inquisitiveness.

When I got home Ae was standing outside my door.

"Hello, Darling," I said.

She rushed to me and threw her arms around my neck and began to kiss me with animalistic fervor, her muscular tongue filling my mouth. When we broke the kiss, she grabbed each side of my head and locked eyes with me.

"Blee, I've thought about you all day. Isn't that strange?"

"I've thought about you, too."

"I want to suck you again," she said.

"Let's get out of the hall," I said with a laugh.

Once inside she was out of her shef before I even put my key on the table. Her underwear was stretched tight across her rectangular body and her nipples looked as if they might burst through the fabric.

"Strip," Ae said.

I laughed. Then I stripped, standing right there in my living room. Ae watched my every move with relish. I was wrong, I thought. She is as curious as anyone. I was foolish to think otherwise. She watched with particular attention when my cock sprang free, already stiff with anticipation. She only shifted when I had removed my last piece of clothing. She pulled her teddy off and threw herself at my feet. She had my cock in her mouth in a flash and soon I was moaning and holding her head and thrusting with my hips. I came a modest amount. She swallowed and kept her mouth around me and grabbed my ass with both hands. She did not disengage until my cock had gone flaccid.

Then she looked up at me. Her beautiful eyes were glassy with fondness.

"Oh, Ae," I said. "Oh, my darling."

"Say it again."

"What? Say what?"

"Darling."

"Darling."

"Ah, Blee. My Blee."

She rose. And kissed me again. I tasted my own halogenic cum in her mouth.

"I've had my dinner," she said. "You must be hungry."

"I could eat you up," I said.

"Oh, my love."

We made some instant food (just add water!) which I had bought at the store. It didn't taste any worse than any other meal I'd had.

"I wish we could watch a movie in bed," I said. I was only half conscious of what I was saying.

"What is a movie?"

"Ah."

This led to a long explanation which led to a discussion about television, books, music (they only had a corrupted doodlebag music that sounded like a drunk elephant), all things alien to her planet. They did have a crude telephone system which worked sometimes and sometimes not. Apparently, the wires were only connected occasionally. Outside of town, I was told, some of the wires lay on the ground where the installers grew tired of their task. They could see no good reason for wanting to contact anyone further away. There was little interest in talking to each other at a distance. We talked a bit about technology, a subject you'd think would stir Ae's soup, so to speak.

"We don't make too many things," she said, simply. "What do we need?"

"Entertainment."

"I don't understand."

"I know you don't, Darling. Are you curious about it? About technologies you have not mastered?"

"Not so much. What do we need?" she repeated.

"The people of your world don't seem to have any curiosity at all."

"I do."

"You more than anyone else."

"I guess that's what led me to science."

"Did you go to school to become a science teacher?"

"In a way."

"What kind of way?"

"I had a teacher. He showed me pictures in books and explained them. We have some science books that have been around since forever. I don't know who drew them."

"Where is your teacher now?"

"He's gone."

"He left Eep?"

"No, he left the world."

"He died."

"Yes. We say he went away."

"Is he buried?"

"Buried? Like in the ground?"

"It is what we do with our dead."

"That's barbaric," Ae said.

"What do you do?"

"Leave the bodies outside of town in the desert."

"I see. But, Ae, tell me more about your schooling."

"He was a kind teacher. His name was Cu. He also was the first man to put his male part inside my female part."

A twinge of jealousy shot through me like dyspepsia. I fought memories of Kalma which threatened to darken my mood.

"He fucked you."

"No. Not like us, Blee. It was science."

"I see."

"I guess it's why I am the curious one. I am very curious about our sex. It is unlike anything that has ever happened to me."

"You're wonderful, Ae."

"I love you, Blee."

This stopped me. I can't imagine what kind of expression I was exhibiting. She loved me? At least they knew love, I thought.

"Do you, Darling?"

"Yes, Blee. That is what we are doing."

"I understand. I love you too, Ae."

"I know," she said. "Can we do some more fucking now?"

"We can, Darling," I said and my heart flooded. Maybe I really did love her. Who's to say?

"Do you know other things about fucking that I don't know?"

"Possibly." I said. I had little experience in outré sexual positions though I knew some things I'd only heard or read about.

"Have you ever been entered from behind?" I asked her.

She wrinkled her mannish nose. "In the hole for excreting?"

"Oh," I said, involuntarily. "That is not what I meant but we could try that too."

She thought a minute. "I am really wet now," she said.

And, so, tonight I took her from behind. Her ass was rather flat but copious and smooth to the touch. I loved petting it as I thrusted in and out. And then I tickled her little clitoris and we had quite a night. I am almost too tired to write this tonight. Ae is sleeping by my side. Who needs curiosity when there is love?

## DAY 29

I have not written for 72 hours. Ae moved in with me and our life, centered mostly on sexual explorations, had little variation, except in the style, place, position and fervor of our sex. I will not record everything we did but I will mention one incident which can represent the entire past three days.

It happened after we moved Ae's things to my apartment. She did not own much. I was learning that on Kepler possessions were not prized. Was it curious that I locked my door? I am not sure. I think crime is practically non-existent but, perhaps, privacy is still much respected. (Plus, many door locks did not work and many keys were so poorly made that they were thrown away.) Ae haphazardly put her belongings where she wanted them.

"Nice, yes, Blee?"

"Yes, Ae. Very nice. I already love having your things here. What will happen with your apartment?"

"Someone else will live there," she said, simply.

"Of course."

"Now, Blee, do we eat or do we bed?"

"How hungry are you?" I asked and smiled.

"Bed," Ae said.

We performed the old ecdysis, eons in the unmaking, across time and space, and kissed for a bit. I relished the feel of her slightly podgy, slightly furred skin against me, head to toe.

"Blee," she said, mouth to mouth. I could tell she'd been thinking about something. "I have an idea."

"Ok, Darling. Is it a scientific idea?"

"It is."

"I am all yours."

"I know Blee. I love you."

"I love you, Ae. What is your scientific idea?"

"I was thinking about the part where I take your dick in my mouth and then I was thinking about the part where you put your mouth over my—what did you call it?"

"Your pussy?"

"My pussy. I like those two parts."

"I do too," I assured her.

"I know. What I was wondering is if we could combine the two. Make it one, um, act."

"69," I told her.

She started. "They are numbered? The things we do. They all have numbers?"

"No, no. This is called 69 because of the shapes of the numbers. They appear to be upside down connected. You see?"

She thought about this for a moment.

"Yes, I see," she said. "I wish I had thought of it."

"It's a wonderful thought. You did think of it."

"I mean I wish I had invented it."

"You don't care about inventions."

"Not things. But acts. Hmm. I will think some more. I bet I can come up with a new act that no one has ever done before."

"It's worth thinking about." I couldn't help smiling.

"So, what we 69?" she said.

"Yes. I think we're gonna like it."

And we did. We liked it very much. Ae came just from the excitement of my ejaculation into her mouth and we had our first simultaneous orgasm. It was quite a night.

## DAY 35

I haven't written in a while. Being with Ae takes up all my time. I have not written a single poem while here on Kepler. I don't care.

Today she whispered in my ear, in the afterglow of another round of gymnastic sex, "We will be married soon."

"Oh, Ae," I answered. "Yes, we should marry. I have never been happier."

"I haven't either. Not even with my teacher."

"What kind of ceremony do we need to prepare?"

"We needn't do anything. One more night in bed and we are married. I think we're supposed to sign a big book in the mayor's office the next day."

"I love the simplicity of Kepler," I said. "A most logical planet."

"I suppose so," Ae said. "Let's do number 43 again."

## DAY 36

Ae and I are married. For the night which cemented it we invented a new sexual position which I will not write down today. For now it seems too private to me. Suffice it to say it got us where we were going and how. Have I mentioned how surprisingly supple Ae is despite the shape of her torso? On Earth she could be an aerialist.

We went to see the Mayor.

"Hello Ae. Hello Blee," he greeted us.

"Mr. Mayor," Ae said.

"I thought it was your time," he said.

"I kept track," Ae answered.

"And the bridegroom. Is he speechless?"

"No, Mr. Mayor," I said. "I am overwhelmed by love."

"Ok," he said. "Sign here."

And we did. And we are wed.

When we got back home I asked Ae where we should honeymoon.

"What is to honeymoon?"

"A ceremonial trip after a wedding. Just the two of us. Some exotic place. Some place you've never been but always wanted to see."

"I don't understand."

"We can go anywhere. Get in a car and just drive. Find a small inn with room service and make love for days."

"We do that here, Blee."

"I know, Love. Do you never take trips? Do you not go anywhere but Eep?"

"Why, Blee?"

"To experience new things."

"Oh."

That was where we left it. We celebrated that night in our usual fashion and well into the next morning. We were both sore and stayed home and ate in bed and I read from *The Spice Box of the Earth* and I tried to make a deck of cards so I could teach her games but I did not have good materials. So, we ate and made love some more.

## DAY 45

We stayed home five straight days until we were both so spent and retted and wrung out we decided it was time to return to the world.

I kissed her a long, warm kiss. "I bet your children miss you when you take time off. Does another teacher sit in?"

"No, no other teachers. There is a math teacher and a spelling teacher. But we don't take each other's children."

"What do your students do when you are not there?"

"Go back home, I guess."

"They must be disappointed."

Ae shrugged. "Some days I have no students anyway."

"What do you do on those days?"

"I just sit in my room."

"You don't talk to the other teachers?"

"No, not on school days."

"What do you do? You can't just sit. You must have books to read, lessons to prepare."

"No, I don't, Blee. Your schools must be different."

"I guess so," I said. But it bugged me. "You must have things to still learn yourself."

"I don't know."

"Plant life, animal life. I know there are animals here. I encountered a rather strange one on my first day in the desert."

I described the lizardy thing to her. She shrugged again. "Poisonous," she said.

"Any idea what that is? How many species are there?"

"I'm sure I don't know, Blee."

"What do you teach then?" I put more heat into it than I intended.

"Science. Bodies and things."

I let it go.

"You can study my body some more tonight," I said in an attempt at lightheartedness.

"Oh yes. We will do that, Blee. We are in love."

All day it niggled me. My coworkers at the garage, typically, did not ask where I had been. I had to tell Ek that I had married Ae.

"Ah, that is a good thing, Blee."

"Yes, she is a fine woman."

"Now you will have children."

It was not a question.

"Yes," I said, thoughtfully. "I suppose we will."

That night I asked Ae, "Do you want children?"

"Blee, we are married. We will have children."

"Oh," I said.

"Soon my body will accept your sperm and a baby will form." She said it the way she might tell one of her students.

"Do you want a son or daughter?" I asked her.

"I'm sure I don't know," she said. "What's to eat?"

"I don't know. Do you want to go to the store and buy some new food?"

"If you want to, Blee."

"Let's do that and then come back and cook and then make love."

"What number do you want to do tonight?" she asked me.

She had taken to numbering our positions and she had a chart in her head that corresponded to various acts.

"You pick," I said.

"I think we've done everything," she said. That same matter-of-fact tone.

"We can re-do things."

"Yes, I like when we do that. I like it better when you invent new things."

"I don't invent, Ae. I only know what I've heard about on Earth."

"Ok," she said. She was thinking. "There must be some things we have not done."

`I did not want to disappoint her. I did not want to tell her that I was not that experienced and that she was, by far, my most inventive lover. "Well, back on Earth there are people called swingers. They sometimes do it with two or more partners."

Ae's eyebrows went up. "Like with three people? Two men and one woman?"

"Or two women," I said. "I am not advocating—"

"I can't picture it but I will think about it. Who would you want?"

"I'm not sure I want anyone else," I said. I felt trapped.

"I will think about another man," she said.

We went to the store and bought some more instant food. Ae was quiet in the car and quiet while we shopped.

"This?" I said. I held up a light brown box. Ae nodded.

Ae was also silent during dinner. Every time I tried to talk I was met with a far-off stare. It gave me great trepidation and I was fearful of what Ae was picturing. We cleaned up the dishes and Ae went and sat on the bed. I was drying my hands and found her there. Her expression said that she was ready to talk.

"There is a male teacher at my school. He might work."

"Ae, I'm not sure about this."

"It would be new. It would be what Earth people do. You want me to be curious."

Had I said that to her? Had she intuited that I was frustrated with her lack of curiosity?

"I've never done it before," I said. I thought that might close the door.

"I'll ask Ji tomorrow. For tonight let's do 69 and then finish it off with some 33."

"Ok, Darling."

I went to sleep tonight with a lot on my mind. Jealousy, that old bugaboo which followed me from my bad marriage, tormented me, and I dreamed that Ae left me and was mating with large lizards in the hot desert sand. I woke sometime during the night and I had peed on myself. I thought, with hope, that I had only had a wet dream, but the truth was more shameful.

## DAY 46

I fretted away most of the morning. I kept picturing this Ji from the school and I was seeing an Adonis, which was absurd, of course. Ji would look just like Ek. He, for that matter, would look a lot like Ae.

"Your mind isn't on your work today," Ek said. It wasn't a reproach. Just a simple statement.

"I know. Sorry,"

Ek shrugged. "Do you want to eat together and talk it over?"

At the lunch break we sat outside on a slight knoll behind the garage. The sun was particularly white today and Ek's lunch looked a lot like my lunch. We chewed meditatively for a while.

"It's our sex life," I said to Ek. He raised his eyebrows.

"Not going well?"

"It is, actually, in spades."

"I don't understand."

"Sorry, an Earth expression. It means very well. Ae and I have been going at it like children with a new toy ever since we got together."

"A new toy. That's interesting," Ek said, blandly.

"We've exhausted every known sexual configuration and ourselves in the process. I've never had so much testosterone. Perhaps it's the air of Kepler."

"So, you've done all eight positions. What is the problem?"

I didn't dare try to explain to Ek that we had practically written our own *Kama Sutra*.

"Ae loves the experiment. I suppose that's a given for a science teacher. I should have been dating science teachers my whole life." I laughed at my own joke and Ek smiled. Ek, like everyone else on this mirthless planet, was a sobersides.

"So, what's the problem?" he asked, kindly.

I hesitated. "Ek, I don't know much about life on Kepler except what I have observed in my time here. I don't know all the mores or whether certain inclinations are in all Keplerites or if individual peccadillos exist."

"I don't—"

I cut him off. "I wonder if you will allow me to talk frankly about sex."

"Of course," Ek said. "Is there a problem on Earth with talking about sex?"

"A bit," I admitted. "A bit. Listen, Ae and I have been, well, experimenting. And she wants to, um, experiment some more."

"Go on."

"Have you ever had more than one lover?"

"I have had many lovers. Before Ig there was Sa, and before Sa—"

"No, I mean at the same time."

Ek thought for a moment. "I have never cheated on my lovers." He still wasn't getting it. "What if Ig wanted to bring another woman into your bed?"

"For what purpose?"

"To have a sexual threesome."

His brow wrinkled for one moment. "Hm. I'm not sure what you're getting at, Blee. Is this something which is common on Earth?"

"I'm not sure how common but it is done."

"Hm. Strange. No. I have never had that experience."

"Or another man?"

"No, assuredly not. Why do this?"

"I can't say for sure, Ek. Pleasure, freedom, experimentation, curiosity." I threw that last word out there. I wanted to break through that wall. For some reason I was becoming obsessed with it.

"I guess we better go do some more cars," Ek said, rising.

"Thank you for talking with me," I told him. I was embarrassed, a bit ashamed.

"We can talk anytime, Blee. Two lovers at once. That's quite humorous," Ek concluded, though he did not chuckle, or snigger, or even smile.

I was home earlier than Ae tonight. This was somewhat unusual because Ae almost always left school in the afternoon. I waited at the kitchen table, reading Leonard Cohen for the tenth time, though absorbing little. She arrived and her face was expressionless.

"Hello, Darling," I said. I hoped my voice betrayed nothing.

"Hello, Husband." She put down her keys and joined me at the table.

"You're late today."

"Yes, I wanted to talk to Ji alone after everyone else had gone home."

"I see," I said.

"So that is what I did."

"What did you talk about?"

"You know. About joining us in our marriage bed."

"I see," I said. My heart was racing.

"I tried to explain it to him. I told him that you said you did it on Earth and that others did it quite regularly and that many found pleasure that way."

"I didn't say—"

"He said he didn't understand."

"Uh huh."

"So, I explained to him some of the things we did and I told him about 69 and other ways of pleasure. He listened quite attentively. Then he said no."

I let out a breath. "He did, did he?"

"I could ask someone else I suppose. But I was surprised that he didn't think it over for very long. I could ask a woman."

"What was his objection?"

"He didn't really say. I tried to entice him by telling him about the length of your penis and about where you had put it. He liked hearing me explain it but he did not want to join us."

"Huh."

"So, I said goodbye to him and asked him what he was doing for the evening and he said he was going to find a woman."

"A woman."

"Yes. And I said, I am a woman. And he smiled and patted my arm and said, 'an unmarried woman. I bet she won't know about this 69 thing'."

Ae seemed downtrodden. She was disappointed and that hurt me. We ate dinner and nothing more was said about a threesome or Ji or about anything sexual. When it was time to turn in for the night I reached for her and we kissed and I touched her and found her pussy dry. I tried to enter her and she wriggled as if she was lying on something scratchy.

"Let me suck you," she said, with little heat.

So, she gave me a blowjob and when I started to come, for the first time, she pulled me out of her mouth and I shot off all over her chest. Then she kissed me and went to sleep. I stayed up for a long time, writing this, and thinking about the future. What did I know of the future?

## DAY 53

I haven't written in a while. My married life has become monotonous fast. I am trying to think of a way to spice it up but I am tired. I am tired of colorless Kepler and I'm tired of the colorless people and I am tired of the routine, the deadly routine. I fear the death of our sex life. I fear that I cannot continue to light a spark in Ae.

We fuck now to make a baby. Every night. To make a baby. This Ae tells me is what a marriage is for. She assures me that soon she will be with child.

Then I thought I should introduce another woman into the bed without telling Ae ahead of time. I fantasized about this for a while but, in the end, it seemed foolish. It would be like bedding twin silkies. It might also queer Ae's family plans. Do I want a child? Will a child make a difference? Will we be happier?

## DAY 75

I'm writing this underneath the blanket because Ae says the light keeps her awake. She told me tonight that I was not doing it right or she would be pregnant. I'd never seen Ae upset before. She has always worn the same placid demeanor everyone on this bland planet wears. I assured her that I was ejaculating correctly. Am I?

## DAY 101

Ae told me tonight that we would not fuck again until we had been to the doctor to have me checked out. I asked her if the problem could be her.

Apparently not.

## DAY 102

The bad news has upset Ae. She is not in bed. I think she is still in the bathroom but she may be asleep on the small bench in the alcove.

## DAY 107

This is the conversation Ae and I had three nights ago.

"Darling, we can still make love. Earthlings make love without desiring pregnancy often. More often than not. Remember our early days. That was something else. Do you want to maybe do 69 or another number?"

"What's the point?"

"Excitement. Love." Maybe I should have said 'love' first.

"If I had known that Earth sperm doesn't mix with ours I would never have—never mind."

"Never have gotten involved with me?"

"I didn't say that."

"You started to."

"I just expected that after all the experimenting we would be making a baby. It's what we do. It's what married people do."

"A little oral sex might change your mind. How about I go down on you?"

"No, not tonight."

"Ae, I love you. This can't be the end."

"It's not the end."

"That's comforting at least. You don't want a divorce."

"A divorce?"

"Ending the marriage."

"We don't have that."

"You don't have divorce? You marry for life? What if the marriage turns out to be an unhappy one?"

"What if?"

"You stay together? Without love?"

"Or children. Marriage is marriage."

"I see."

"I'm going to sleep in the alcove tonight."

"Ae, I love you. Please come to bed."

"I love you, too. Good night."

"Ae," I said, with some heat. "I need sex. I need you." Perhaps I should have said 'you' first.

"Tomorrow I'll give you a hand job. You will be happy you taught me that."

"I can give myself a handjob."

Ae wrinkled her nose. "What?"

"Yes, I can masturbate. It's not as satisfying."

"What is masturbate? You can have an orgasm without me?"

"Of course."

"Show me."

"No, Ae. Come on. This is absurd."

"Show me the masturbate and I will think about the other."

So, I did. To my shame, I pulled it out and stroked it to orgasm while Ae watched with her best science teacher's inquisitiveness. When I came her eyes widened.

"Hm," she said. "And that is pleasurable?"

"Not as much. Not as good as sex with you, Darling." I was wheedling. I was using a wheedling voice while the semen ran down my stomach and beneath my scrotum.

"Can women do that?"

"Of course, Ae, but—"

And that was that. She has not returned to the bed since. Tonight, I heard her cry out, "OH MY!" And I put my face in my hands and wept.

## DAY 120

At the garage today a woman brought her car in because it was making a loud noise 'right beneath her feet.' I promised her I'd look at it right away. She smiled a Giaconda smile and went to sit on the grass behind the garage.

The noise beneath her feet was a small, hard-shelled animal gripping the car's undercarriage for dear life. It had claws like mechanical pincers. I called Ek over to have a look at it.

"Look at that," Ek said.

"What is it?"

"Some kind of small animal. Desert I'd say."

"Yes, I know. But what kind? Is it dangerous?"

"Who knows? It's not doing the car any harm really. I'd tell her that."

"Ok," I said. I summoned the woman into the garage and she joined me underneath her car.

"Yech," she said. "What is that?"

"Have you been driving in the desert?"

"Yes, I just returned from Vum."

"Where is Vum?" I smiled as I asked.

"Across the desert," she said. "Can you get that thing off the car?"

"I'll try," I said. "Why were you in Vum?"

"My sister lives there."

"She moved there from Eep?"

"Yes," she said.

She returned to the grass and I asked Ek and another mechanic to help me pry the little monster off the car. We managed to get a crowbar under it and an oil pan beneath it. I counted to three and when we applied pressure to the bar the creature screamed. It sounded like a female victim in a slasher film. Ek dropped the pan and the other mechanic let go of the bar and backed away quickly. I found myself face to face with the little bastard which now had a crowbar stuck in its ribs. It looked at me with animalistic malevolence. I was not afraid. What difference would it make if the thing bit me and I died? No one would mourn. And I would be free of myself, Ae and Kepler 1647b. I pulled the crowbar out of its ribs and bashed it once in the face. It fell to the ground underneath the car and was obviously dead.

"Look what Blee did," Ek said with admiration.

I smiled a tight smile and walked out of the garage.

I got in my car and drove toward the desert. I was either going to Vum or to kill myself. Or both.

## DAY 121

Obviously I didn't kill myself. Instead I drove all the way to Vum. It took me the rest of the day. I found a small inn that looked like the small inn in Eep and the small inn in Remp. I ate in the restaurant. I showered in the tiny stall. I wrote in this diary. I slept and dreamed I was back on Earth in the pot store and there were young women everywhere and they all had perfect human bodies and I wept in my dream and when I woke I was still weeping.

This morning in Vum I went for a walk. There was nothing to see.

I drove back to Eep and at home that night Ae greeted me and kissed my cheek. She did not ask me why I did not come home the previous evening. As I am writing this I can hear Ae's nighttime self-pleasuring. I want to kill her.

## DAY 133

After work this evening I wrote a new poem. It's not the only thing I've written on Kepler but I think it's the best. I've always admired poets who grappled with the everyday but, when the everyday is on another planet, this becomes a dilemma. So, I wrote about Ae. Not a love poem exactly but not *not* a love poem. A sex poem I guess one could say. I venture to say that no one in the history of poetry had ever written such a poem, about entering the body of a hairy alien and teaching that alien about sexual pleasures she had never dreamed of. Not even Yeats had that much imagination.

## DAY 155

Something terrible has happened in Eep. Everyone is masturbating. Ae, of course, told someone about what I had taught her. That someone told someone else. And now it is a craze. And they are not doing it in the privacy of their homes. They are doing it everywhere, whenever the urge strikes them. In the grocery store, in their cars, leaning against any building.

At the garage, at least once a day, one of the mechanics drops his shef and beats off. No one even turns around.

"That was a good one," one of the mechanics said to me after he had finished. "Thanks for that."

I am getting patted on the back repeatedly. They believe I have brought them this gift from Earth.

Another day that same mechanic took one of the female clients out back and they both masturbated. As she drove away from the garage she stuck her head out and thanked me.

I am thinking about suicide again.

## DAY 157

This morning Ae kissed me with a little more fervor than usual.

"Husband, have a good day at the garage," she said. "You are all anyone is talking about. I am very proud to be your wife."

I thought about that all day. Ek asked me how my marriage was going. I told him that it was floundering and that I felt lost and alone on their planet.

"I understand," Ek said. "I was telling Ig last night about how popular you are in town because of the new thing you have taught us."

"Ek, I never meant to teach anyone anything."

"I don't understand. But Ig said something interesting. She said that she wondered if this masturbation craze would hurt marriages, would hurt our planet's procreation. What if our generation is the penultimate?"

"I hardly think that possible, Ek. Lovers still will want to make love."

Ek was thinking about this so I added, "It hasn't affected you and Ig, has it?"

"The past few nights we have not made love. We only masturbated."

"Is that uncommon? I mean, the part about not making love for a few nights."

"We make love every night. We are married."

"Then perhaps you are the luckiest planet in the solar system, if in the solar system you are."

"I don't understand."

"I know, Ek."

That night Ae had a little lilt to her step. When I got home she had made dinner, such as it was, and put the bottle of Bik in the center of the table. We had not drunk Bik for a long time.

"Hello, Husband," Ae said and kissed me wetly.

"Darling, why is the Bik out?"

"I thought you needed a treat. You've seemed down lately."

"You've noticed." The sarcasm was lost on her.

"Yes, Husband. Why don't we have a little Bik with dinner and see where the night goes?"

I was all aboard for this. I had a semi-erection.

So, we ate and drank a bit and chatted about our jobs.

"We have a new teacher at the school. He's from out of town, way out of town. I had not even heard of his town before. He was sent here because he did something bad in his own town. He was forced to leave by the populace."

"What had he done?"

"I don't know."

"No one asked?" I knew the answer.

"No, no one asked. Ef's going to teach sex."

"Sex," I said.

"Yes, sex."

"How is he going to teach sex?"

"Well he came here to teach exercise but as soon as he heard about masturbation he decided that he would teach that. He said he's just learned how to do it himself. The mayor showed him when he greeted his arrival. And then Ef asked me to show him how a woman does it."

"And you did."

"And I did."

"Oh, Ae," I said, just as a purple and orange pyrotechnic exploded behind my brow.

"Husband," Ae sighed. It sounded a lot like love that sigh.

"Ae, can we go to bed now?"

"Husband I am so proud of you that I thought I could start sleeping in our bed again."

"Nothing would please me more," I said.

So, we left the dishes dirty and undressed each other quickly. The bik was bubbling inside me. My head was full of fulguration and my cock began to swell like forgiveness. When Ae took down my underwear she looked at my cock as if it had been a long time. It had been a long time.

"I forgot how big you are."

"Oh, Ae," I said. I was almost delirious with desire.

"You're much bigger than the new sex teacher. Maybe I should suggest he use you for the class."

I almost lost my buzz.

"Lie next to me, Husband."

I joined her on the bed and we lay side by side. I put one arm over her and began to move my body toward hers.

"Watch this," she said. And she patted her clitoral area with a series of sharp, short slaps. And then she called out, "AHHH!" and her body shook. When she was through she opened her eyes and looked at me. "Good, yes?" she said. She had a twinkle in her eye.

"Yes, lovely," I said, because it was.

"Now you," she said.

"Yes, take it," I said.

"No, Love. Now you masturbate."

I was dumbstruck.

"Ae, I want to fuck you," I said with some heat.

"This is better, isn't it?"

"It is not."

"It is better for me. I come much harder. The new teacher said he did, too."

"Fuck the new teacher," I said.

"I don't need to," she answered.

I am thinking again about killing myself.

## DAY 186

The masturbation craze continues. Ae and I are sleeping in the same bed. Sometimes we do it missionary style. It does not overly excite either of us. She assured me that my gift to their world was the most exhilarating thing they'd ever experienced.

## DAY 225

Masturbators are beginning to tire of the activity. At least I hope so. I see fewer of them in public places. As for Ae and me, our lives are as colorless as this colorless planet and as tasteless as its food.

## DAY 244

Ae has moved back to the alcove. She does not masturbate as much, she tells me, because none of it feels that stimulating anymore. She says she's heard the same thing from other teachers. Originally, they had formed a masturbating circle and spent their breaks together getting off in the communal room. The attendance started to drop off until finally only she and the new teacher, Ef were left. After masturbating together for about a week they decided to start fucking. Ae said, with a melancholic tone, that it was no good. She could not get wet and Ef could not come.

## DAY 275

Something is afoot. I have heard discontented rumblings among the townsfolk and my coworkers at the garage are not talking to me. A dolor has covered the town like a fog. Denizens are walking around without greeting each other, their sadness palpable, their anger barely under the surface.

Ae won't talk to me.

## DAY 301

Ae told me this morning that there was a movement among the populace to punish me for what I've done to them.

"What are you talking about, now that you've chosen to talk to me again?" I said with some acerbity.

"Masturbation has cursed our town, and other towns from what I have heard, and you are being blamed, of course. There have been no pregnancies in months and married couples are not sleeping together anymore. The discontent has spread to the children who have become unruly and wild."

"Maybe your town needed shaking up," I said. I was sorry I said it.

"Why have you done this, Blee?" Ae's voice broke my heart. She seemed genuinely distressed, genuinely defeated.

"Ae, I did not mean to do anything except love you and have you as my wife for all time."

"But you brought us this black magic. It is worse than any war."

"Have you had wars?"

"I'm not sure. Some people think there were wars a long time ago."

"Then I don't think the phrase is appropriate."

Ae looked at me as if I were something under her microscope, if she had a microscope.

"Ae," I then said. "I am sure that this is only temporary. Why don't you and I reinvigorate our sex life and perhaps our example will spread for the good just like it did for the evil."

"Then you admit your fault?"

"I admit nothing. I am fishing for a way to keep you and to save the town."

`Ae looked dubious "By reinstituting the perverted ways you taught me which have poisoned our people?"

I was shocked speechless. "Perverted?" I managed after a few moments. Where had she heard the word?

"You are a sick alien and you have brought your sickness to us."

Tonight, Ae did not come home.

## DAY 302

They came this morning and arrested me. I have been placed in a cell, ten feet by ten feet. It is not exactly a jail because they did not have a jail. I am in an old storeroom down the hall from the mayor's office. Their lone police officer, Ze, deputized Ek and Ig and the three of them formed the arresting troop. They allowed me to keep everything I brought with me, my writing stuff, my Leonard Cohen, which is falling apart, its leaves dropping as sad as autumn. Perhaps it is autumn.

I think I've lost a poem or two.

I asked them if there was to be a trial.

"I don't understand," Officer Ze said.

"Skip it," I said.

"Ok," Officer Ze said.

"How long is my sentence?"

"Five words. Is this a trick?" he responded.

"How long will I be in jail?"

"There is no escape," he assured me.

"Not escape. How long until you let me go?"

He said, "I don't understand."

## DAY 322

The food here is worse than the food outside. I did not think it possible.

There is no break, no exercise.

There is a nice toilet and sink. Best thing about Kepler: their facilities. Of course, I shit regularly, I have since I began living here, and my excreta is the same color as the food when it goes in. Worst thing about Kepler: the food. And the tedium.

I lie and dream. I dream about Earth, its multi-hued beauty, its changes, its piebald occurrences. I hallucinate in Technicolor.

I dream about Kalma. Her lips, her eyes, her rump, and legs. And I masturbate over her. She is all that arouses me now. Because she is lost. Because I have lost her and the world. Because my life is over and I can now say that she is all I ever loved. Losing her was the first loss, the one that led to the others. I lost the world while I was still on Earth.

O, Earth. How I long to see you one more time.

## DAY 365

If my calculations are correct I have been on this planet for one year.

My incarceration continues. No one visits. No one talks to me. The woman (I think it's a woman) who brings my food keeps her eyes averted as she slides my tray in. She will not answer any of my entreaties or attempts at colloquy.

I am utterly alone.

My pencil is a nub I sharpen with my teeth.

I am at the end. This must be the end. I am alone at the end.

## DAY 4000

I am non-spirit. I am thewless.

I am the dirt under my nails.

I am visited by insects, small creatures shaped like Earth women. They taunt me with their tiny sexes.

I am.
Still I am.

## DAY ZERO

I am nil. I am negation.

I am starting over.

I am scratching this along the sides of my last fragment of paper.

I am the breast, the babe, the life.

I have been born again, as heat and dust. As subhuman.

## DAY 1.1

They've left me in the desert. They tired of feeding me.

I am surrounded by emptiness, ugly greige emptiness. Dry as a caldron full of hammers.

I am here a god. I am God. THE.

I write this on my shoe. It is barely legible in the dirt, the grime that is part me and part this horrible world.

I will die now. I will die God's death as it has been predicted and practiced over and over. I am God dying. This is God's power, this pageant, this Golgotha, this Easter.

The sun is white and so high. I am blind. I can only see the sun, a white spot on a monochrome background.

I am starving, dying with only vinegar on my lips.

I will carve my last words in my own flesh.

Take me home. I am through now.

# POSTLUDE:

## THE RETURN OF THE SON TO THE FATHER

The white void of the sun began its descent shortly after daybreak. I watched it make its slow progression toward me. I felt at peace. As it neared it did not get hotter but the bright light was almost blinding.

When it rested a few yards above the surface, about 50 yards from me, I waited for what it would bring. A figure began to take shape at its center. It was a man, an Earthman.

He sat cross-legged. He was dressed in many colors like a saint. His face was kind, a radiant smile set against the soft hair of his smooth whiskers. He did not speak but his smile was for me.

"Are you Shiva?" I asked.

"You do not need Shiva," he answered in an orphic voice. It was like flute music.

"No?"

"No, you are Shiva."

"Are you a god of Kepler 1647b?"

"Again, you do not need a god."

"We all need gods."

"Perhaps. But in the Now you only need me."

"I am listening."

"I am listening as well. You may talk."

I was stymied. I had been through so much yet I could not think of a thing I wanted to talk about with this Being of Light, be he god or swamp gas. I thought for a long time and he kept very still, a beatific grin on his face that looked oddly familiar.

"I don't know how I got here."

"Do you know how you got anywhere?"

I wanted more than this. I wanted enlightenment. I wanted comfort.

"This planet is insane. It's boring and—awful."

"Yet here you are."

I thought about this. I wanted to say something positive.

"Their toilets are ingenious."

The being flickered. I thought I was losing reception. I was wearying him away.

Quickly, I said, "I still miss my wife. I still miss Kalma."

"She still misses you."

"Will I go back to her then? Have you come to take me home?"

"I am not a celestial hack."

"Will I see her again?"

"Not on Earth."

"Shit. Then why are we talking?"

"Why *are* we talking, Billy?"

"It's good to hear my name again."

"We need our names, perhaps more than we need our gods."

"I am Billy Kos."

"That's right."

"Tell me your name, Spirit."

"I have the same name as you."

"You are me, or I?"

"In a sense."

"Are you my father?"

Now he smiled a real smile, an Earthling's smile. He looked like a heavenly hippie, his golden hair rolled to his shoulders like the Christ's. He nodded slowly, and the light wavered. I was transfixed.

"Where do I go from here?" I asked, after a while.

"You will go where you are supposed to go. You will be what you are supposed to be. And, finally, you will be Camel and Camel will be you."

I looked long and hard at him. The surrounding desert shillyshallied beneath me, receding. He sat in his bubble of light and smiled.

I smiled, too. And, I said my final words. Three. Simple. Words.

"I don't understand."

*Sit finis libri, non finis quaerendi:* "Here ends the book, but not the searching."

(Photo credit: Sandra Smith-McDougall.)

**COREY MESLER** has been published in numerous anthologies and journals including *Poetry, Gargoyle, Five Points, Good Poems American Places,* and *New Stories from the South*. He has published nine novels, four short story collections, five full-length poetry collections, and a dozen chapbooks. His novel, *Memphis Movie*, attracted kind words from Ann Beattie, Peter Coyote, and William Hjorstberg, among others. He's been nominated for the Pushcart many times, and three of his poems were chosen for Garrison Keillor's Writer's Almanac. He also wrote the screenplay for *We Go On*, which won The Memphis Film Prize in 2017. With his wife he runs a 144 year-old bookstore in Memphis. He can be found at https://coreymesler.wordpress.com.

## BOOKS BY COREY MESLER

### Poetry

*For Toby, Everything for Toby* (1997) Wing & The Wheel Press
*Ten Poets* (1999) editor, only Wing & The Wheel Press
*Piecework* (2000) Wing & The Wheel Press
*Chin-Chin in Eden* (2003) Still Waters Press
*Dark on Purpose* (2004) Little Poem Press
*The Hole in Sleep* (2006) Wood Works Press
*The Agoraphobe's Pandiculations* (2006) Little Poem Press
*The Lita Conversation* (2006) Southern Hum
*The Chloe Poems* (2007) Maverick Duck Press
*Some Identity Problems* (2007) Foothills Publishing
*Pictures from Lang and Fellini* (2007) Sheltering Pines Press
*Grit* (2008) Amsterdam Press
*The Tense Past* (2010) Flutter Press
*Before the Great Troubling* (2011) Unbound Content
*Mitmensch* (2011) Folded Word Press
*The Heart is Open* (2011) Right Hand Pointing
*To Writing You* (2012) Origami Poems Project
*Our Locust Years* (2013) Unbound Content
*My Father is Still Dying* (2013) Flutter Press
*Body* (2013) Chapbook Journal
*The Catastrophe of my Personality* (2014) Blue Hour Press
*The Sky Needs More Work* (2014) Upper Rubber Boot Books
*The Medicament Predicament* (2015) Redneck Press
*Stone* (2015) Origami Poems (chapbook)
*Opaque Melodies that Would Bug Most People* (2015) After the Pause Books
*Mountain* (2015) Fairfield Press
*Home* (2016) Fairfield Press
*Among the Mensans* (Iris Press) 2017
*River* (Fairfield Press) 2018
*Madstones* (Blaze/VOX Books) 2018

## Prose

*Talk: A Novel in Dialogue* (2002) Livingston Press
*We Are Billion-Year-Old Carbon* (2005) Livingston Press
*Short Story and Other Short Stories* (2006) Parallel Press
*Following Richard Brautigan* (chapbook) (2006) Plan B Press
*Publisher* (2007) Writers Write Journal Press
*Listen: 29 Short Conversations* (2009) Brown Paper Press
*The Ballad of the Two Tom Mores* (2010) Bronx River Press
*Following Richard Brautigan* (full-length novel) (2010) Livingston Press
*Notes toward the Story and Other Stories* (2011) Aqueous Books
*Gardner Remembers* (2011) Pocketful of Scoundrel
*I'll Give You Something to Cry About* (2011) Queen's Ferry Press
*Frank Comma and the Time-Slip* (2012) Wapshott Press
*The Travels of Cocoa Poem Lorry* (2013) Leaf Garden Press
*Diddy-Wah-Diddy: A Beale Street Suite* (2013) Ampersand Press
*As a Child: Stories* (2014) MadHat Press
*Memphis Movie* (2015) Soft Skull Press
*Robert Walker* (2016) Livingston Press

www.ingramcontent.com/pod-product-compliance
Lightning Source LLC
Chambersburg PA
CBHW070452120726
47910CB00003B/1025

*9780999671641*